I0586992

A Time of Times

T. R. Healy

TAILWINDS PRESS

Tailwinds Press
P.O. Box 2283, Radio City Station
New York, NY 10101-2283
www.tailwindspress.com

Published in the United States of America
ISBN: 978-0-9975742-4-1
1st ed. 2019

"What then is time? If no one asks me I know: if I wish to explain it to one that asks I know not."

– Saint Augustine, *Confessions*

A Time
of Times

Part 1

Time In

The Ecstasy of the Animals

The blue Chrysler slowed down in front of the sloped driveway. Jess Rudyard hurried across the lawn and crawled into the back seat beside Kevin, who was clawing an electric razor across his dimpled chin. He greeted everyone perfunctorily, searching for some place among the papers and bottles on the floor to set his long legs. He was the last one in the car pool to be picked up when Silas drove and he paid the price, but with Max he was the first, able to sit in the front with plenty of leg room.

"By the way," Kevin said, pulling out of his briefcase a small package wrapped in silver paper, "Kate said I should give you this." He handed the package to Jess. Max turned around inquisitively, and Silas looked up in the rearview mirror.

"What is it?" Jess asked, surprised.

"Open it up and find out."

Eagerly he tore the wrapping to shreds and found a can of foot powder. "Just what I need."

Kevin laughed, then handed a similar package to Max to give to Silas. "Sorry," he said to Max. "No gifts for those who refuse to see the light." He laughed again, louder.

Max smiled. "Thanks, but I can wash my own feet."

The others, active members of the same church, were selected to be apostles on Maundy Thursday, which, as part of the service, required them to have their feet washed on the altar by Monsignor Greer. Both Silas and Kevin had been apostles in the past, but this would be the first time for Jess, who had moved into the parish less than eight months ago. Silas and Kevin, conspiring behind his back, had volunteered his services as one of the twelve, which he wished now he had refused. Time and again, he found himself in some corner, having to do something he had no wish to do, yet foolishly he complied, pulling on another mask. He was always making himself up, assuming strange attitudes and postures to accommodate others, and he supposed Thursday would be no different. He had grown accustomed to being told what to do, forever the pupil, probably because of his cautious father, who had impressed on him the wisdom of following the example of others, believing it wise to do only what had already been done.

"Some advice," Silas said to Jess in a serious tone of voice. "Be sure and trim your toenails. Last year, one of the celebrants snagged his thumb on a nasty hangnail of Brian Sheed's."

"That could have been very toxic," Kevin cracked, "considering all the beer he drinks."

They laughed heartily, their shoulders shaking. Jess kept his silence, wishing he had never agreed to participate in such nonsense, while Kevin went on to detail all the attention he gave to his feet the first time he was selected to be an apostle, wanting them to appear as clean and polished as a new pair of shoes.

Silas glanced around. "Now you know why he often

has his foot in his mouth. He's keeping it clean."

They circled the turnaround, passed the church, and proceeded toward the stone gates that marked the entrance to the neighborhood. Within a block of the gates, Silas reduced his speed and all of them glanced down the narrow street on their right, craning their necks as they crawled through the intersection. The object of their attention was the yellow house in the middle of the block with the rusted camper in the driveway.

"It's probably a pupil of hers," Silas said, referring to the piano teacher who lived in the house.

"She must really like this one," Max observed.

"She'd like a leper if he rang her doorbell," Silas snarled.

Through the gates, they continued toward the river, down the increasingly busy thoroughfare, sharing their surprise about the camper being in the driveway three mornings in a row. Seldom, since they began riding together some six months ago, had they noticed the same vehicle parked in her driveway for more than two mornings. None of them knew the piano teacher, although Silas suspected someone at his lodge might; he thought he recognized the guy's car, a black Impala, in her driveway one morning.

A slight woman with tangled hair touched Jess on the thigh and asked the time. He looked at his watch. "Twelve minutes after seven."

"It's always twelve minutes after something."

"Somewhere."

Coyly she traced a finger along the lapel of her silk blouse, revealing a glimpse of her left breast. "You look familiar."

He regarded her a minute. "Rome?"

"Never."

"Cabo San Lucas, last summer?"

She shook her head.

Jess smiled at the slight woman who was his wife, Alma. They were waiting in a pale hospital lounge for their friends, the Stengels, who had invited the Rudyards to accompany them on a tour of the maternity ward. Sometimes, for no reason, they pretended to be strangers meeting one another for the first time and casually introduced themselves, sometimes making up imaginary identities. More and more, it seemed, they were playing the charade, gradually becoming more intimate in their pretenses than they were as husband and wife. After the Stengels arrived, they went upstairs to the maternity ward, where the nursing supervisor conducted them and half a dozen other couples around the area. All the couples except for Jess and Alma were prospective parents who had been encouraged by their obstetricians to visit the ward, so they would be more at ease when they came to deliver their babies. For Jess and Alma, however, it was another night out; they often spent several nights out during the week, as Alma, dreading sitting in front of the television as Jess was inclined to do, always tried to arrange somewhere to go in the evening. Indeed, if he didn't know better, he might have suspected she had arranged for him to be an apostle.

When they got home he handed Alma the house key and walked down to the corner to mail a letter. He moved slowly, deliberately, breathing deeply. All the talk tonight of having children had depressed him. He needed to get away for a while, to stretch his legs, and walked past the mailbox and crossed the street. Sometimes, at home, he felt as if a heavy curtain had collapsed over him so that he could scarcely move, and then all he wanted to do was leave.

It was a clear, crisp night with a slight breeze. He turned up the collar of his jacket and drew the lapels together. Across the dark blue sky, a panther stretched its massive limbs and slowly swallowed the moon. He passed the Swallows, beginning the short climb up the hill, passed the Sheeds and Blums. Through the large front window he watched Meg Blum wind away from her husband in a slow turn, then swirl under his arm as he led her around the room. They slid past one another, randomly, like leaves in the street. A trike belonging to one of their daughters lay on its side, blocking the sidewalk. He stepped over it and, for a moment, imagined he was stepping into his future, surrounded by the glare of television screens, toys on the lawn, couples dancing in their windows. Soon, he knew, he would be just like them, and the thought startled him, causing his right shoulder to twitch. Certainly many of his neighbors were very fine people, with qualities he wished he possessed, but he wanted to be different in some way, not just another forgettable member of the community. He suspected the brief stint he spent in the seminary after high school was not out of any deep conviction to become a priest so much as it was to do something different from his friends, to set himself apart by going in another direction.

At the end of the climb he stopped and drew a long, slow breath. Ahead of him, in the distance, stood the stone gates. He was surprised, not realizing he had walked that far. He crossed the street and then, as he did every morning on his way to work, he glanced over at the yellow house on his right. It was too dark to make out the driveway so he turned and started down the street, squinting. He was practically in front of the house before he spotted the red Fairlane in her driveway, just like the one, he thought, owned by Calvin Hanratty, an usher at the eleven o'clock Sunday service. Then, before he realized what he was doing, he found himself on her porch, peering in the window.

It was dark and all he could see was his own reflection, so he crept along to a lighted window on the side of the house. There he found a small olive room where a television shone that no one was watching. He continued along, from window to window, looking for another light, when he heard voices from somewhere inside the house. He began to go around, then all of a sudden a light came on in the house next door and a heavy woman in a quilted robe drifted past a window, carrying a basket of laundry in her arms. He leaned back, retrieving his breath, and waited until she was gone. Then her porch light came on, the door scraped open, she was coming out, he realized, and instantly he streaked down the driveway, clipping his hand against the side of the car. Somewhere a dog barked furiously. He ran as hard as he could, feeling ridiculous, wondering what the neighbors would think if they could see him running across their immaculate lawns.

Silas swerved through the turnaround too sharply, causing his passengers to slide toward him, grumbling. Kevin pretended to open the door as if to walk to work, and Silas, laughing, eased to a crawl as they approached the stone gates.

"I don't recall that one being there before," Max remarked, spotting the Fairlane.

"Me, either," Henry said, staring.

Silas grunted. "I can't keep track anymore."

"Calvin Hanratty owns a Fairlane, I believe," Jess said hesitantly, thinking about last night.

"You don't think he's in there?"

"He wouldn't dare," Kevin declared.

"I thought his car was green, not red," Max said.

"Let's have a look," Silas suggested, turning down the street and driving slowly past the yellow house. All of them looked at the car carefully, their faces pressed to the window like postage stamps.

"It's someone else's," Max said, pointing out that Calvin's familiar fish emblem was not pasted on the bumper.

"Jesus, though, can you imagine if it had been him?" Kevin wondered aloud. "He'd have been the talk of the parish."

They laughed as they passed through the gates.

That evening a practice was scheduled at the church for the designated apostles. Driving there, Jess noticed the driveway of the piano teacher's house was vacant, so on an impulse he pulled in and walked up to the front door. He was determined to see what she looked like up close because rarely was she ever outside when he rode to work, and then only for a moment, stepping into a car or through a doorway. He considered various excuses for pressing her doorbell, but when she answered he explained that he saw her sign in the window and was interested in registering for some piano lessons.

"I took some for a couple of years as a youngster," he said, "but I never progressed much beyond a lame rendition of 'Maple Leaf Rag.'"

She was trim and delicate, a little older than he expected, somewhere in her thirties, with loose brown hair and hazel eyes. Abruptly she swung open the screen, sweeping her hair over her left shoulder. "Here, let me see your hands." She whisked them out of his pockets like gloves, looked at them, turned them over, pressed down on the knuckles. "Firm but delicate," she assessed pertly, still holding them.

He felt the blood glowing in his cheeks, then suddenly turned her hands over, stared at her long fingers, stroking them gently. "Firm and sensitive," he replied.

She grinned and drew away her hands. "I have an appointment soon, but if you'd like to, you could come in and play something, to see what level of lessons you should begin at."

He declined, explaining that he had to be going, but made an appointment at the end of next week, which he knew he would not keep. He had satisfied his curiosity, that was all he cared about, so he left for the practice, convinced she would fade from his memory as quickly as he could pronounce his name.

At the practice he forgot all about her, dutifully concentrating on making sure he grasped all the details of the Thursday service. Walter, a layman who performed various functions at the church, from unlocking doors to reading the epistle at the weekday Mass, presided over the practice. He had attended numerous Last Suppers, having been raised in the parish. Promptly at eight he assembled everyone into the east end of the church to march down the aisle in procession and divided them into two files according to height. One of the men, a novice like Jess, wondered if they would represent particular apostles. Smiling, Walter explained how at one time they used to select names out of a hat, but because no one wanted to be Judas, they quit and now everyone was anonymous.

"Except you," Silas interjected. "You have to be Peter. You're in charge."

Walter touched his temple and then led them down the aisle to the back of the altar. They sauntered through the dark church as if they were out on the playground, talking loudly, laughing, clad in jackets and sweaters and scuffed tennis shoes. A tin of unconsecrated communion wafers pilfered from the sacristy was passed among them as they sat on the long wooden benches around the altar, listening to Walter explain different aspects of the service, in particular the mandatum. His remarks were crisp and to the point, designed to make sure the laymen comported themselves on the altar with the utmost dignity. A few of them, cracking jokes, expressed their unease about the washing of their feet, but Walter emphasized it was an example of fellowship that had been set for the apostles to follow, and urged that the men should approach the ceremony accordingly, citing John from memory: " 'A servant is not greater than his master, nor a messenger than the one who sent him.' "

The twelve apostles stood at the back of the church, in a dim hallway, waiting for the service to begin. They were dressed in starched white surplices and long black cassocks, like the servers and singers at the front of the procession. In all, there were a couple dozen people packed in the hallway. The smell of candle wax and smoke, from the burning torches the acolytes held, permeated the air.

Silas, slumped in a corner at the top of the stairs, furtively offered his cigarette to Kevin, who took a long drag. Walter eyed them closely as they passed the cigarette between them.

"My prayerbones are already beginning to ache," Kevin complained, massaging his knees.

"I'm melting with all these clothes on," Jess groused.

Silas agreed, fanning his face with his fingers. "I almost wish they had assigned us names, and I were Judas, so I could get out of this damn thing."

Kevin laughed. "Be careful what you wish for, you may get it."

In another moment, the altar bell rang. "Time, gentlemen," the Monsignor intoned, straightening his stole. Docilely everyone in the hallway stirred into place, the torches were raised, the choir began to sing. The procession, in a slow, somber curve, followed the crossbearer down the center aisle past the congregation and wound around the altar, slowly coming apart as everyone went to his station. The apostles, as in the practice the night before, occupied the long benches at either end of the communion rail, sitting erect, with their hands on their knees, as Walter instructed.

"There's my wife," Kevin whispered, nudging Jess in the ribs. "On the left, three rows down."

Jess glanced at the pallid woman smiling at her husband. He surveyed the large congregation, bowed in prayer, and spotted his next door neighbor on the aisle near the side entrance. Alma was not in attendance, she was at a shower for Evelyn Stengel. Idly he gazed down the aisle again, past the confessionals, past the large Riordan family, to Calvin Hanratty who stood behind the offertory table, holding in his hands the wicker collection baskets. He was a pillar of the parish, someone the Monsignor was almost as dependent upon as Walter. The notion of his car being parked overnight at the piano teacher's made Jess smile to himself. For if it had been his Fairlane, half the parish would know about it by the following Sunday. Jess pictured the faces of the congregation then, full of derision and contempt. Poor Calvin, he thought, a pillar in pieces.

The Host was raised, the bell rang three times, then the chalice was raised and the bell rang three more times.

Jess closed his eyes, not in prayer but in reflection, trying to imagine himself on the altar consecrating the bread and wine. The image now seemed as fanciful as the notion of Calvin spending the night at the piano teacher's. He remembered, one afternoon at the seminary, deciding he had no desire to enter heaven but preferred to remain in purgatory, where he could be at ease and out of the sight of God. At first it was only an amusement he shared with some other seminarians, but then he began to take it more seriously until it became a sincere ambition. Because his motive for entering the seminary was to serve himself, not others, he was not surprised when he left, but still he regretted his failure to become a priest and wished now he had never tried. He believed, after his experience at the seminary, it was probably better not to try something than to fail; perhaps that was why purgatory had become his ambition: it was less of a chance.

At the end of the service a wooden clapper was shaken, and the apostles assembled in front of the communion gate in their bare feet. Slowly, one by one, they filed past the silver bowl of water on the bottom step of the altar. Jess was the fourth apostle to pass. The subdeacon gripped his right foot firmly while the Monsignor washed and kissed the foot, mumbling a prayer. He thought how silly he was to worry about the ceremony as he stepped away, one foot cool, one dry, on the hardwood floor.

The supper was generous and authentic, consisting of wine, roasted lamb, and unleavened bread. The apostles sat with the Monsignor at a long table in the basement, surrounded by card tables patronized by members of the congregation. Everyone, according to custom, ate with their fingers, rinsing them in bowls of warm lemon water. After the supper, Jess went with Silas and Kevin to an oyster bar downtown, where they celebrated the end of their discipleship by taking a trip around the world. The oyster bar offered beers from nearly everywhere in the world, and at a special price encouraged its customers to make the journey.

"Where to first?" Silas asked.

Kevin swiveled on his stool. "The Old Sod of course."

Silas, grinning, ordered three glasses of Guinness.

They followed the itinerary of an old train rumbling across Europe—through the Lowlands, over the Alps, to the edge of the Black Sea—then through the Orient. At each stop they exchanged toasts and then resumed their reminiscences about favorite old baseball teams as if they were in Silas' car driving to work. All they ever talked about were games they played and games they watched. The service that evening was just another game, distracting them from themselves. Jess felt as if he were going in a circle, moving from one distraction to another in the same still orbit. He tried to imagine himself again as a priest, aware that he had no desire to assume such responsibilities, but like a priest he wanted to cast his shadow on the altar. He believed he had to be noticed to acquire an identity; otherwise he was not even there, a transparent figure.

After leaving the Orient they returned home, ordering Coors, which they consumed in a few swallows, then wobbled out to their cars, still exchanging toasts and laughing. They raced one another out of the parking lot, then headed in separate directions. Jess, a little light-headed, drove cautiously past the shipyards, over the narrow suspension bridge, down a violet street glaring with advertisements. In the morning, going to work, he often travelled along part of that street, but at night he hardly recognized it, and for an instant wondered if he had made a wrong turn and anxiously stared across the windshield, searching for something he remembered seeing in the morning. He felt adrift, lost in his own neighborhood; suddenly his home seemed farther away than ever. Then, after a few more blocks, one as strange as the other, he spied the stone gates in the distance and steered toward them, moving down a street strewn with broken branches.

Through the gates, he cruised past the piano teacher's, saw the driveway was clear, and circled the block, pulling into the driveway the second time he approached the house. He switched off the ignition and darkened the headlights, having no idea why he was there, and every idea. He sat for a minute, listening to the engine tick like a clock. Gradually he imagined himself as someone else, as Calvin even, someone whose car he might have seen in the driveway before, and became that person, shedding his apprehensions, and strode up to the front door.

He woke early the next morning, in plenty of time to return home to make up an explanation and dress for work, but he continued to lie in bed with the piano teacher curled against his back, her hands resting against his shoulder. She stirred slightly, still asleep. He looked at her a moment, her loose hair spread across her face, and listened to her slow breathing. Soon, he thought, the Chrysler would be approaching the gates, and his friends craning their necks, and he could imagine the astonishment on their faces when they saw his car in the driveway, and all the snide remarks they would exchange. By the end of the day, no doubt, scores of people would know what happened, including Alma, and he knew he should move his car, but he left it there. And calmly lay waiting for them to come, figuring he had finally acquired an identity in the neighborhood.

Downtime

It was so quiet that for a moment the dogs next door began to bark furiously, as if something were the matter.

Alma also was surprised not to hear the familiar growl of jackhammers this morning, the whine of electric saws and the shouts of workmen. Something indeed must be the matter, she thought, as she eased into her bathwater. Ever since she discovered that the old Dakota Building was going to be demolished, she had worried that something unforeseen might happen. Despite the assurances of her husband and neighbors, despite all the precautions taken by the people in charge, she remained on edge as the blast day approached, still expecting something to go wrong.

"You just can't blow up a building in the middle of a residential neighborhood," she told her husband, "and not expect some damage to occur."

Soon the hammering resumed, silencing the barking dogs, and impulsively Alma plugged her fingers in her ears. For nearly a week now she had been listening to that racket coming from the Dakota Building, hour after hour until she thought her ears were going to burn off. It would all be over by the end of the week, the building reduced to rubble and dust, and she just hoped she could hold on until then without going to pieces herself.

The Dakota Building, a relic of red stone and barred windows, was for many years an apartment house for older people in the neighborhood. No one had resided there for several months, however, since it was sold late last summer to some developers from Canada who planned to build a large office park in its place.

"It's hard to believe the Dakota isn't going to be standing there after Sunday," the mailman said to Jess as they stood across the street from the ramshackle building. "One of my aunts used to live there before she passed away, and I can remember many a Sunday afternoon visiting her there."

Jess nodded pensively. "The place has been there a long time, all right. About as long as anyone around here can remember."

"I understand it's supposed to drop in a matter of a few seconds."

"In the blink of an eye from what I've been told."

"It's hard to believe," the mailman said again as he resumed his route.

Jess removed his old baseball jersey, which was streaked with sweat, then bent over the sawing trestle and cut another large piece of plywood. He was standing in the driveway of old lady Coble's house, sawing and stacking wood that later he would fit over her front windows to protect them from incurring any damage from the blast. Along with several other people in the neighborhood, he had agreed to put up scaffolding for the homes of the older residents who were located within the immediate vicinity of the Dakota Building. He had taken off the past three days from work to gather blisters the size of raspberries on his hands.

Usually he worked alone but sometimes Midge stopped by in the afternoon, not to help but to talk. He and Jess had met in the Army while being trained in demolitions. That was almost nine years ago, and they had not seen one another since then until Jess happened to recognize his old acquaintance the other week at the Dakota Building and identified himself. Midge remembered him after a moment, smiled and shook his hand, and quickly they disclosed what they had been up to since their discharge.

"I'm still in the smithereens business," Midge admitted, explaining that for the past year and a half he had been working for the general demolition contractor on the Dakota project.

"I always figured you enjoyed blowing things up a little too much."

He chuckled. "To be honest, Jess, it's the money I make that helps me retain my enthusiasm for the work. But I can't deny I still get a kick out of dropping something big like the Dakota."

"This is the first time a structure of this size has ever been demolished with explosives inside the city limits."

"So I understand," he said. "I guess this really puts your little neighborhood on the map."

Jess nodded. "Thousands of people are expected to be out here to watch the blast."

"All the attention we get is what makes our work so different from what you and I did as soldiers. Now I sometimes feel as if I'm part of a circus that has come to town. People pester me with questions, ask to have their picture taken with me, ask for my autograph, offer to buy me a drink or take me out to dinner. It's incredible."

"The daring young man on the flying trapeze, are you now?"

He laughed. "Believe me, Jess, we get the royal treatment practically wherever we go. And you know what, chum? It feels great."

"I bet it does," Jess replied, also laughing.

"You ought to try it sometime," he cackled. "Hell, everybody ought to have the chance to be in the spotlight at least once in their lives."

"Guess what?" Jess asked his wife as he rushed into the kitchen where she was rinsing a bowl of strawberries.

"What?"

"I saw a ghost today... someone I haven't seen in years. We were in the Army together."

"What's your friend doing here?" she smiled. "Haunting some old house or something?"

"You could say that, I guess. He's here to blow up the Dakota."

"You'd think he'd've had enough of that sort of work in the Army?"

"This isn't the same thing at all, Alma," Jess insisted. "He's the toast of the town these days, not some raggedy soldier anymore."

Throughout dinner Jess talked about Midge so much that he almost seemed to be an invisible guest at the table. He recounted some of the projects Midge had told him he had worked on, marveling at all of the different places his friend had visited in the country and at the enthusiastic reception he had received in many of those places. Midge was as much of a celebrity, he told his wife, as that fellow in Texas who puts out oil fires all around the world.

"He scarcely knows anything more about explosives than I do," Jess said, "yet he's regarded as some kind of wizard, if you will."

You could be him, Alma thought to herself, knowing exactly what was going through her husband's mind this moment. You could be crisscrossing the country, earning pocketfuls of money and being treated like someone special if you didn't have to be stuck here with your pregnant wife.

The more Jess went on about his old Army acquaintance, the more suspicious she became that he was going to leave with him after the blast on Sunday. Ever since she became pregnant Alma had expected Jess to go away again, unable to accept the responsibility of finally settling down and raising a family. She had always assumed he would leave her for another woman, not to blow up buildings, but one served the same purpose as the other, she supposed, so long as his independence wasn't threatened.

She would not be able to track him down this time, she knew, she was too far along in her pregnancy to be wandering all over the place. She had become as slow as an old woman during the past month, breathing heavily just climbing up the stairs. She grimaced a moment, recalling the long drive she had made last time in search of Jess, finding him barely conscious in a dreary little lounge at the coast with a woman twice his age. This time, if he left, she feared he would be gone forever.

Late on Friday afternoon, two days before the blast, Midge invited Jess to accompany him as he supervised the loading of explosive charges on the cast iron columns in the basement and on the first floor of the Dakota Building. They proceeded cautiously through the restricted area, through all the rubble from the walls that had already been knocked down by the workers, slowly circling the exposed columns. They had been trained in the service to demolish targets without regard to the effects of the blast, but the demolition this Sunday had been designed to minimize the damage to other property in the neighborhood.

"If you kick the supports out of a building," Midge reminded Jess, "the only way it can go is down."

Jess remembered. "Kill the body and the head dies."

"There you go, chum."

After a moment, Midge paused before a column on the first floor and looked at Jess, smiling tautly. "Do you want to decorate this tree?"

"Are you serious?"

"Sure, why not? You're qualified. You received the same demolition training as I did."

"All right, if you say so."

"I say so."

Jess mounted the stepladder beside the column, then helped another worker secure the explosive charge to the side of the column. Surprisingly he was relaxed, sure of himself after all these years.

"It appears you've still got the knack for this kind of work."

He nodded. "It's like riding a bicycle: once you learn you never forget."

"I guess you learned well, Jess. I guess both of us did."

For the past three years, Jess had been sitting at his desk on Friday afternoons, sipping a mug of coffee, sorting through and reviewing different policy claims, and not once had he ever experienced this kind of satisfaction in his work. He felt at this moment as if he had really been doing something that mattered, not simply putting in time until it was five o'clock and he could go home. Suddenly he considered the possibility of leaving the insurance business and going to work for Midge on a regular basis, even though he knew Alma would object, not wanting him to be on the road all the time and fearing he might become injured working with explosives. He tried to shake the idea from his thoughts but it remained there, like a dull ache at the back of his head.

That evening, at dinner, Jess told Alma that he had been invited inside the Dakota the night before the blast to help Midge attach the firing mechanisms to the explosive charges. He was barely able to contain his enthusiasm as he told her, nervously tapping his steak knife against the edge of the table. "He also invited me to watch the blast with him from the command post," he said.

"I'd assumed you were going to watch it with me?"

He looked at her, his face clouded with confusion. "I didn't know you were really interested in watching it. You never acted as if you were."

"Maybe you weren't listening to me, Jess."

"Oh, I was listening all right. I was listening with both ears, and you weren't showing the slightest bit of interest until just now."

She swung her legs out from under the kitchen table, leaning back a little in her chair. "You really want to go, don't you?"

"Well, I told Midge I'd help him out, and I don't see any reason to renege now."

Her eyes sizzled in anger. "I mean, Jess, you want to go away from here...from me...from this child of yours I am carrying."

"Don't be ridiculous."

"I know you, Jess. You'd leave with your Army friend in a heartbeat if he asked you because you find things here too small and confining."

Jess slumped in his chair, his shoulders turning in as if he were suddenly being embraced by someone. "I can't deny I've thought about it, sure. But it's not because I want to leave you or the child. It's because I believe I could provide a better life for us with the money I'd be making with Midge."

"This time if you go," she fumed, "don't expect me to be coming after you. Not this time, Jess."

"Oh, don't be ridiculous," he said again, wondering if she might be right after all.

It was dusk. The first floor of the Dakota Building was almost as dark as the basement. Carefully workers crept across the dusty floor, making the final preparations for the implosion tomorrow morning.

Jess, holding a flashlight, watched as Midge rigged a firing mechanism to the base of another column, considering to himself whether he really wanted to go to work for Midge as he had speculated the other afternoon. He thought so but he wasn't sure. Obviously the demolitions business didn't promise to make him rich or famous, but it did offer at least the prospect of gaining the sort of attention and prosperity he could never gain working in an insurance office. If not a step into the spotlight, he thought, it was at least a step out of the shadows.

Moments later, as they moved on to rig another column, a worker came up to Midge. "We've had an unexpected visitor, boss."

Midge sighed with irritation. "Who is it now? Another neighbor trying to take pictures of the inside of the building?"

"Not quite, boss," the man grinned. "A kid was spotted climbing the fence at the north end and throwing something into the building."

"What was it?"

"He said it was just a stick so we checked it out, but instead of a stick we found a dead snake."

"What?"

The man laughed hoarsely. "At first the kid denied he threw it but after a little persuasion he admitted the snake was his pet."

"So why in the hell did he throw it into the building?"

"Because he wanted to give it a memorable burial, he said."

Midge glanced at Jess, shaking his head. "You think you've heard it all, then something like this happens."

"What do you want me to do with the snake?"

"Let it lie," he laughed. "And tomorrow morning it'll have the most memorable burial that kid could have ever hoped for. Under six stories of dust."

"You're the boss."

Midge proceeded to another column, still laughing about the incident with Jess, who continued to hold the flashlight as Midge installed another firing mechanism.

Time passed slowly, and as it did Jess recalled an instructor he and Midge had in training who used to tell them before they began a field exercise, "Now get out there, troops, and make some memories." He was still trying to carry out that order, he supposed. Otherwise why else was he here tonight with Midge, if not to make some memories, like the boy with the snake. He regarded the preparations for the demolition as a chance to revive some of the special moments he had shared with Midge in the service. But he was only fooling himself; he knew the past could not be repeated. Now it was necessary to make some new memories, and thinking of the child Alma was carrying, he was confident the future would be full of such memories.

"It's time to go," Jess said as he touched his wife on the shoulder.

She rolled over on her side, groaning softly.

"It's time for the big bang everyone's been waiting for," he whispered.

She rubbed her eyes. "I thought you were going to watch it with your Army friend."

"I changed my mind," he said tersely. "Now let's get a move on. Rise and shine."

It was still dark out but already the streets were filled with spectators, pressed as close as possible to the barriers that had been set up to cordon off the immediate area of the blast site. By the time Alma and Jess had made their way to the porch of one of their neighbors around the block, however, a sliver of sunlight began to appear through the clouds. Strings of balloons were visible from some of the surrounding houses, along with carpets that had been hung in the windows as protection against the blast. And to their right rose the Dakota Building, appearing as if it would be there forever.

A warning siren was sounded at the two-minute mark, which was greeted with a chorus of cheers and whistles from the crowd.

Alma, startled by the siren, edged closer to Jess. "Don't you wish you were up closer to the front now?"

He shook his head as the siren issued another warning. "I can see everything just as well from right here."

"You're sure?"

He gripped her wrist, gently stroking her hand. "I'm positive."

Then, with fifteen seconds to go, the siren sounded for the last time.

"Here we go, everybody," someone shouted anxiously from the driveway. "Hold on tight."

Suddenly then, after what sounded like an enormous drum being beaten, the old building shuddered and collapsed in a black cloud of dust. At once there were cheers and shouts from the thousands of spectators. Some also rang bells and blew horns, as if it were New Year's Eve.

"It fell so quickly," Alma marveled. "Like a house of cards."

"It's always faster to tear something down than it is to put it up."

"So it seems."

Jess stared at the thick cloud of dust that had already begun to envelop the crowd. "Alma, I'm sorry."

"For what?"

"For ever thinking of going away with Midge. I didn't mean to upset you. Honestly, I didn't."

She pressed a finger against his lips. "Let's not talk about it anymore. That's all in the past, Jess, just like the Dakota Building."

The Pedestrian

The blades of the bamboo rake scraped across the pavement as Alma turned to watch Mr. Ambrose cross the street. He seemed to move in spurts, as if coaxed by the wind, heading toward the footbridge as usual.

"The walking overcoat," Mrs. Treece cracked, stepping from behind the hedge separating their driveways. "I was on my way out when I saw him coming across the playground so I waited in the garage until he passed. I know that isn't right, but I didn't want to get stuck listening to him go on about Mrs. Ambrose again."

Alma, silent, resumed her raking.

"I'm surprised he didn't corner you," she continued. "He always corners me."

"I was behind the side of the chimney."

"You saw him coming too?"

"Yes," she admitted in embarrassment.

"You have to hide from him, otherwise you'll have to listen to him complain again about the length of his wife's illness and the cost of her treatment. About the fact that no one was there to administer the last sacraments to her in time. My word, Alma, that was more than a year ago."

"Not quite."

"Well, almost," she snapped. "He can't expect a person to feel sorry for him forever."

"I suppose. But I hate to dodge him all the time."

"So do I."

"He must know we're doing it."

"Perhaps. But there's a limit to everything. Even sympathy."

Alma leaned forward on the rake, raising a hand against the sunlight.

"Before he lost his wife he seldom left his house," Mrs. Treece remarked. "But now every morning, like clockwork, he's out the door."

"I wonder where he goes every day."

"Lord knows."

Out raking again, early the next morning, Alma watched for Mr. Ambrose, and after he turned the corner and headed toward the footbridge, she began to follow him, walking on the opposite side of the street. But after a few blocks she grew short of breath and had to stop. The old fellow, momentarily bitten from view by a passing school-bus, had more than doubled the distance between them. She was amazed she had not been able to keep up with him, considering that she was almost young enough to be his granddaughter.

A couple of days later, having purchased a sturdy pair of leather walking shoes she found on sale, she tried again. And once again she failed to keep up with him. Later that evening, while the boys and her husband watched television, she sat in the bathroom, soaking her feet in Epsom salts. It reminded her of last fall when she was canvassing the neighborhood, handing out "Pick Nick" pamphlets in support of a candidate for the school board, and strained a calf muscle and spent nearly a week soaking it in salt water. Now that both her sons were in school, she often left as soon as they did, dreading staying home alone. She canvassed for assorted candidates, was a member of numerous organizations and guilds, and worked on behalf of many charities. Mr. Ambrose was simply one more excuse for getting out of the house, she supposed, although she had become curious about where he went every day. Still, it was careless of her to follow him in new shoes without breaking them in first. So for the rest of the week, while her blisters healed, she wrapped each shoe in a towel and pounded it for several minutes with a wooden mallet, slowly softening the leather.

On Monday, in a cold drizzle, she was able to keep the old fellow in sight until he disappeared down a narrow alley behind the lumberyard. He had moved ahead of her as though she were walking in sand. In frustration she kicked a decapitated rocking horse lying in the alley, causing it to shiver as if carrying a rider.

The next morning, over coffee with Miss Laurel, her next door neighbor, Alma watched the old mountain goat shuffle down the street, trailed only by the lean terrier that belonged to some children around the corner. Miss Laurel had known him longer than anyone else in the neighborhood, so Alma asked her where she thought he was going every day.

"Nowhere, really," she speculated.

"But he must be going somewhere. He leaves the house every day."

"He just goes out in the neighborhood." She stirred a spoonful of sugar into her coffee, slowly. "Walking his dog."

"I didn't know he had a dog."

She touched a finger to her forehead. "The black dog," she said. "Up here. Ever since Mrs. Ambrose died, he began going out, as if the memories in the house were making him leave."

Next door, at the Tydings, they heard a telephone ringing in the kitchen.

"Mind you," Miss Laurel continued, "I've never cared for the man, personally, on account of his ill disposition and the awful stories he'd try to tell me sometimes. But naturally I feel sorry about what happened to Mrs. Ambrose. However, walking the streets isn't any sort of solution because you're still carrying the problem with you. Up here," she said, again tapping her forehead.

Alma conceded that she was not in any condition to keep pace with Mr. Ambrose. So every afternoon she began to go for a walk through the neighborhood, hoping to develop enough strength and endurance to stay with him one of these days. At first she confined her excursions to a few blocks around her house, gradually increasing her distance as she grew stronger and less winded.

"You look so haggard, dear," Mrs. Wicks remarked to Alma one afternoon as she returned from one of her longer walks.

"I've been out walking."

"Is something wrong with your car?"

She smiled and patted her middle. "I need the exercise."

"You're skin and bones."

"And starch," she laughed, drawing a pinch of skin from her waist.

Even though Alma had resided in the neighborhood for almost six years, involving herself in as many activities as any of her neighbors, she quickly discovered that she had scarcely any knowledge of it beyond the houses along her street. Now, as she walked, she saw all sorts of things that she had failed to notice when she was driving by in her car. It was as if she were in another end of town, acquainting herself with an entirely different neighborhood. Just a few blocks from her house, behind the water tower, she found a cracked swimming pool sprawling with weeds. She discovered a tarnished plaque in a wild blackberry patch, commemorating some neglected pioneer. She passed a faith healer with a brass cross fastened to his front door, and a palmist who advertised her skills on a banner sagging above her porch. There was a grove of chestnut trees behind a nursing home, where she gathered handfuls of fallen nuts to take home to roast. Once in the grove she nearly jumped out of her skin when a German shepherd suddenly cornered her, barking viciously.

Another afternoon, crossing the playground, she spied a mail carrier on the opposite side of the street and, on an impulse, attempted to keep up with him as he made his deliveries. A white house a blue one a brick one another white house. Block after block. Excitedly, as the carrier moved toward each house, she slapped her thigh, delighted as she kept pace with his long, loping strides. Soon, she told herself, she would also be staying with Mr. Ambrose.

Eventually she was walking as far as the extinct volcano at the very edge of the neighborhood, where she liked to test herself over its steep terrain. The climb became an important feature of her walks, helping her to develop the stamina that was necessary if she hoped to keep up with Mr. Ambrose. And one afternoon, as evidence of her increasing strength, she managed to elude a young man she thought was following her along one of the trails on the volcano. At two different crosspaths he went in the same direction she went, always remaining a short distance behind her. Not wanting to take any chances, she headed straight for the summit and gradually he disappeared as she made her way to the top.

That evening, in bed, she told her husband about what occurred at the volcano.

"Did he say anything to you?" Jess asked, concerned. "Did he try to do anything?"

She shook her head while removing a pin from her hair.

"Really, you have to be so careful walking around by yourself, Alma. You never know who you'll cross paths with these days. The streets are full of strange people even in our neighborhood."

She beamed. "The guy couldn't catch me."

Jess regarded her with a sidelong glance, waiting for her to elaborate on her remark.

"I was too strong for him," she said proudly. "I went up to the summit and he just faded away. He couldn't keep up with me."

Jess, rolling over on his side, was silent.

"I'm in the best condition of my life," she declared. "Just feel the backs of my legs, the muscles in my calves and thighs."

He lay still, falling asleep, his eyes closed, his hands tucked beneath his pillow.

"Here, feel," she insisted and scraped one of her

callused heels against his skin.

"Don't."

"Jealous?" she taunted, pinching his domed stomach.

"Quit it!" he snapped. "It's stupid, if you ask me, walking all over creation. The neighbors must think you're getting as touched as old Ambrose down the street."

She stabbed her pillow. "Fat chance."

Alma pulled on her legwarmers, fastened the snaps of her anorak, then stood at the kitchen window and waited for Mr. Ambrose. Today she had decided to follow the old fellow again, convinced that she was finally in condition to keep up with him. Anxiously she stared out at the empty street, hardly able to contain herself, she was so eager to get started.

A few minutes later, through the branches of the birch tree on the corner, she spotted him shambling down the street with a newspaper rolled under his arm. Instinctively she signed herself with the cross, praying she would not fail this time, then hurried out the back door as soon as Mr. Ambrose started across the street. She took long strides as he descended toward the footbridge, and by the crosslight had reduced the distance between them to approximately half a block. For a split instant, as he waited for the light to change, the old fellow glanced over his shoulder. Quickly she turned her head and slid into a shadow until he continued ahead, past more old houses and apartment buildings.

At the lumberyard, where she had lost him the last time, she remained strong and broke into a broad smile as she trailed him up the footbridge. She was not superstitious, but still she was careful to avoid stepping on any cracks in the pavement, not wanting to try her luck. He would have to walk her into the ground before she quit this time, she assured herself. She would not stop until he stopped.

Across the bridge she followed the old fellow to a shopping mall where she approached within a few feet of him, not wanting to lose him in the crowd. Slowly he meandered through the mall, often pausing in front of the different shops to look at their glittering window displays. So this was how he spent his days, Alma thought to herself irritably. She shouldn't have been so surprised, she supposed, since Miss Laurel had suggested to her that he probably went out every day to escape the memories his house held of his late wife.

Gradually, as she stalked him past the shops, she recognized the foolishness of what she was doing. Even so, she continued to follow him, recognizing that like the old fellow she was also searching for an excuse to avoid staying home by herself. She knew, in her heart, that she was not really that interested in Mr. Ambrose, and as her attention wandered she suddenly imagined others in the mall she could follow instead of the old fellow. To her right was a tall, graying man with a bulging briefcase who she thought might be a lawyer and lead her somewhere interesting, like a courtroom. Behind him was a woman with snapping green eyes, and next to her another woman whose stunning long legs turned several men's heads. And coming toward Alma was a West Indian in dreadlocks who, she was sure, could take her to a corner of the city she had never been to before.

I could follow whoever strikes my fancy, she thought, just step right behind them and lead their lives for a little while. Almost anyone's seemed preferable to her own numbing existence at times.

At length, the old fellow stepped into Newberry's, and instinctively she also entered the crowded store and trailed him down a long aisle of men's toiletries. She expected him to wander aimlessly through the store, but instead he paused before a shelf of cologne and, before she knew it, slipped a bottle of English Leather into the pocket of his overcoat. She was shocked, scarcely believing what she had just observed. Immediately she looked around to see if anyone else saw what happened, but there was only one other person in the vicinity, an elderly woman whose attention was focused on a tray of lipsticks. Mr. Ambrose, meanwhile, proceeded down the aisle, and Alma quickly trailed behind him, wondering to herself if she should report what he did to a clerk. Surely someone else must have spotted him and he would be arrested before he left the store, she thought, deciding not to say anything, but he walked out without anyone laying a hand on him.

Alma remained confused as she followed the old fellow out of the mall. She could not believe he couldn't afford to pay for the cologne, knowing that he received an ample pension from the postal service where he had worked for so many years. It could not have cost more than some pocket change. So what compelled him to take it, she wondered, if he had the money?

The next morning, confused as ever, Alma followed Mr. Ambrose back to the shopping mall. For almost an hour, the old fellow wandered from shop to shop, bending before one window after another, before he finally set foot inside a large sporting goods store that was having a clearance sale. He was there only a matter of moments before he pocketed an expensive pair of swim goggles. Alma, astonished, was certain he would be caught this time, but again he walked safely out of the store.

By the next day, when she followed Mr. Ambrose into a pharmacy and watched him slip a small hair brush into his overcoat, she was hardly surprised at all. By then she had almost come to expect him to take something whenever he entered a store. Still, she remained puzzled by his stealing, unable to determine why he put himself in such jeopardy for such trivial items. He never took anything that he appeared to need, certainly never anything he could not afford to purchase. Perhaps he was simply taking the things out of spite, she speculated, perhaps it was his way of adding some edge to his otherwise dull existence without his wife. In a sense, she supposed, she was scarcely any different, because she had become his virtual shadow the past few days mainly to provide some excitement to her own drab routine.

They were two of a kind, she decided, mere shadows on the street.

As she continued to follow Mr. Ambrose, she grew more concerned about him, about the possibility of his being arrested someday. When she trailed him into a store she almost regarded herself as his secret accomplice, watching out for clerks and security guards who presented a threat to him. More than once, when she thought he was going to slip something into his pocket, she blocked off an approaching clerk with some superfluous question about his merchandise. Curiously she found herself becoming as excited as Mr. Ambrose must have felt when he took something without being caught. She felt almost buoyant at times as she followed him out of the store, secretly sharing in his defiance of rules and regulations.

One morning at Newberry's, after the old fellow had swiped a large brass belt buckle from a rack of buckles, he was detained by a store clerk just as he started out the door. Alma, startled, froze for a moment. She had noticed the clerk standing near the doorway, but she could not believe he had seen Mr. Ambrose take the buckle. He was too far away, she thought. He was probably only engaging in some small talk, she figured, asking the old fellow how he was feeling or if he thought it was going to snow this weekend. Then, suddenly, she saw Mr. Ambrose unbutton his overcoat and the clerk remove from one of the side pockets the stolen belt buckle.

Oh, Christ, she swore to herself. Christ . . . Christ . . .

Briefly the clerk glanced around and his eye caught hers. At once she thought he was going to detain her as an accomplice. Shivering, she turned and followed a Chinese customer out one of the rear doors, not for a moment daring to look back at the old fellow and the store clerk. She walked briskly, resolutely, her arms pumping at her sides, as if she were climbing one of the winding trails on the volcano.

Adamantly, as she crossed the parking lot, she reprimanded herself for having been so foolish as to have followed Mr. Ambrose in the first place, scarcely realizing that she was still following the customer she had trailed out of the store.

Showtime

Vaguely, as he stood on the corner, Jess began to have the feeling that he was being watched, and after a few moments he looked around but did not recognize anyone in the cluster of people scattered along the sidewalk. He looked back, deriding himself. He was forever having inklings of things about to happen that seldom ever occurred. Still the suspicion persisted, and a moment later he looked around again, but everyone seemed to be looking down the street at the approaching parade. About a hundred people proceeded through the intersection behind a large banner that read "Take Back The Night," chanting and carrying candles. Jess searched intently for the two young women from the office who told him they would be in the march tonight to protest the spate of assaults on women that had taken place downtown over the last few months. Just the other week an exchange student from Nigeria had been attacked in one of the tiered parking lots as she was unlocking the door to her car. Recently Jess and some of the other men in the office had agreed to serve as escorts and walk the women to their cars and bus stops. At first only a few accepted their offer, but after the last attack several more had asked to be escorted from the office building. Jess had walked someone every night that week.

Near the middle of the procession were the two women from the office, and as they passed Jess they shouted his name and raised closed fists, grinning broadly. He waved back, clenching his fist.

"I love parades."

Startled, Jess turned, and at his side was an unshaven man in a soiled overcoat and a blue watch cap.

"Doesn't matter really what they're marching for. I just love to stand and watch a parade go by. I guess it makes me feel like a kid again. You know what I mean, mister?"

"Actually, I've never cared much for parades as a youngster or now," Jess said coldly. He turned away then, trying to ignore the stranger.

"Here, let me introduce myself. My name is Jess."

Jess looked at him curiously. "So is mine."

"Oh, what a coincidence," he exclaimed. "I'm Jess Rudyard."

Jess was incredulous. "I don't believe it. You can't be."

"Cross my heart," he said, crossing himself.

Immediately Jess felt for his wallet, thinking the man had picked his pocket, then he noticed the letter sticking out of his breast pocket. "You saw my name on this letter, didn't you?"

The man seemed confused, annoyed. "I didn't see any letter. My name is Jess Rudyard. What is so strange about that?"

Jess was convinced now that the man had spied his name on the letter. He suspected he would be asking him for money next so he began to walk away behind the parade.

"Where are you going, mister?" the man asked. "I thought maybe we could have a cup of coffee together... get to know one another."

Jess grew tense, could feel his heart throbbing beneath his coat, and began to walk faster through the crowd. He wished suddenly he had an escort now. At the corner he started to turn around to see if the man was following him, but dashed instead into the street and ran to his car. There, breathless, he locked his door and sank his head into his hands. His fingers were trembling, making his head shake like a closed fist. Tightly he gripped them against his scalp until they were still, then drove home.

"Well, you know what they say: everybody has someone they look like, somewhere," Alma remarked after Jess told her about the man he met at the parade with his name.

Jess frowned at his wife. "For Christ's sake, he was short and scraggly and all stooped over like an old man. He looked like a refugee. He was in rags. He didn't bear the slightest resemblance to me, not the slightest."

"But he had your name," she said, standing on her toes, practicing a step she had learned the other night at her ballet class.

"I told you, Alma, he must've seen it on the letter sticking out of my pocket. Or else heard those women from the office calling me."

"I know, dear. I'm only teasing."

"But why would anyone do such a stupid thing? What's the purpose saying he was me? It makes no sense."

She spread out her arms and spun slowly across the kitchen. "Even so, the strangest things happen sometimes," she said after a moment, collapsing on her heels.

"Everyone, at one time or another, has thought of someone they haven't seen in ages and, a day later, they turn a corner and there that person is. Almost as if they willed it to happen." She stood back on her toes again, lifted out one leg and extended it across the breakfast counter like a roll of bread.

"I can assure you, Alma, I was not thinking about meeting that man at the parade tonight. Although I did have the feeling a few minutes before he appeared that someone was staring at me."

"See," she said, as though everything had been resolved.

He thought a moment. "No, actually, I don't see anything."

Later, getting ready for bed, Alma reminded him of the experience of her cousin who had married someone with the same birthday as hers, divorced him, then married another person with the exact same birthday.

"So?"

"So you can see the strangest things can happen. The only sense they make is that they happen."

Jess ignored her, resolving to forget about tonight. What he could not explain, he decided, was better forgotten.

Tobie faked his father with his shoulder, then jumped into the air and shot. The basketball rattled off the backboard through the torn net. Jess picked it up, dribbling to his left. The boy and his father charged up and down the narrow driveway, silent and intent, trading baskets. Dark rings of sweat spread across the backs of their shirts. A few years ago, Jess had attached the basket to the front of his garage, and whenever he felt at loose ends with himself he would go outside and shoot baskets for half an hour. But playing a game was always more fun, and he was glad whenever Tobie or one of the boys in the neighborhood came behind the house to play against him. He seldom beat any of them but he enjoyed the workout, feeling the blood circulating through his veins, breathing hard, feeling half his age.

Pivoting, Jess started toward the basket when he saw the man from the parade last night coming up the driveway. Dumbfounded, he paused and stared at him while Tobie deftly tapped the ball out of his hands and laid it in the basket.

"Hello, mister," the man said, touching a smudged finger to his temple. "Mind if I watch?"

Jess ignored him and tried to continue the game, but his concentration wavered as he wondered what the man was doing here, and Tobie easily scored the next three baskets to win the game.

"You look tired, mister," the man said after Jess sent Tobie inside the house. "Sore bones like us are getting too old to be playing games anymore." He laughed hoarsely, clawing at his collar.

"Who are you?" Jess snapped at him. "What do you want from me?"

"Don't you know me?"

"All I know is that your name isn't Jess Rudyard."

A faint smile appeared at the corners of his mouth. "We went to grammar school together."

Jess regarded the scraggly little man closely, trying to remember back almost thirty years to when he was in grammar school.

"You don't remember me, do you?"

"I'm sorry. I don't."

The man glowered at him a moment, then stooped down and picked up three chestnuts from the ground. Softly he clicked them together in his hands, threw one above his head then another, and began to juggle the three chestnuts.

"Penny!" Jess exclaimed in recognition.

The juggler bowed, with a taut smile, and tossed a fourth chestnut into the air. Jess remembered him as being the cleverest boy at school, forever juggling things, playing card tricks, making coins disappear into thin air. He had been a couple of years ahead of Jess, but Jess knew him from all the times he had performed at school assemblies and on the playground during recess. He was the perpetual entertainer, never able to resist performing his wizardry if he had an audience.

"I wondered if you'd remember me. Some folks don't."

"Well, Penny, it's been over twenty years."

"True, but I recognize them," he declared. "Just as I recognized you last night when I saw you at the parade."

"And I'm surprised," Jess admitted, patting his small belly. "I've changed quite a lot since then, like forty pounds worth."

He shook his long hair. "No, Jess, you haven't changed. Not like some folks . . . not like me. You're the same all right. If you weren't you wouldn't be recognized now, would you?"

"Oh, I'm not so sure, Penny."

"I am," he snarled, staring at the circling chestnuts. "Then folks you remembered wouldn't remember you or want to remember you. Believe me."

Jess watched him juggle the chestnuts, marveling at his

skill. He was still as impressive as he had been at school. Jess had always been so awkward with his hands, even now playing basketball with his son, that he inordinately admired anyone who displayed the least amount of dexterity. But he also felt sorry for his old friend. Plainly, from his appearance, he had been through some thin times. His hair was shaggy, he had not shaved for several days, his overcoat was splotched with coffee stains, his shoes scuffed as the pavement. He could easily imagine people from Penny's past slighting him if they recognized him on the street. Indeed, though he did not recognize him until he began juggling, Jess had done as much last night, believing Penny to be a beggar, and he was ashamed. He had been slighted a few times by people he knew, and he understood how demeaning it made someone feel, as though he suffered from a terrible deformity. He hated people who had done that to him, and he hated himself for doing it last night. And he swore to make amends to his old friend.

As it was getting chilly, Jess invited Penny inside his house and heated some coffee, found a basket of walnuts in the pantry and sliced some cheese and rye bread, which Penny devoured as if he had not eaten in a week. Although he did not want to embarrass him, Jess inquired what he was doing these days, thinking perhaps he needed some money. He was eager to help now after being so rude to him last night.

"Oh, I'm doing my tricks as usual," he said. "But the days are growing colder now so pretty soon I'll have to come inside and find some work until spring."

He explained that for almost eight years he had worked as a truant officer for the school district. Then one afternoon, after apprehending a schoolboy whom he found juggling apples on a streetcorner for pocket money, he made up his mind to do something he enjoyed for a change, and a week later he left and became truant himself. He had not performed any of his tricks in years but gradually, with a lot of practice, he regained his skills until one afternoon he was able to stand on a streetcorner and entertain a crowd and have his hat sparkle with change. He had been juggling for his living now for a little over two years.

"You probably think I'm wasting my life away?"

"Not if you enjoy what you're doing, I don't."

"Oh, I do, Jess. Juggling is something I can do well, what makes me different from other people. You can't imagine how good it makes me feel to be surrounded by a crowd of complete strangers, making them laugh, hearing their applause. People are so appreciative then. Oh, sure, there is someone in every crowd who has a look of ridicule in his eyes, as if to say how pathetic it is to see someone at my age still standing on streetcorners, but those people can never understand the satisfaction I get from performing my tricks."

"You can't please everyone."

Penny nodded. "It's never hard to spot those people and, believe me, when I do I stop whatever I'm doing and stare right back at them until they walk away with their tails between their legs. The weaklings." He laughed fiercely, bitterly, rapping his fist on the counter.

They reminisced a while about different people they had known at school. Finishing his coffee, Jess excused himself and went upstairs to shower. Waiting, Penny walked out to the garden and amused himself by balancing a rake on his forehead. When Alma returned home from the grocery store she was startled to find Penny on her front lawn, surrounded by several children, and rushed upstairs to tell Jess that a tramp was trespassing on their property.

"He's not a tramp," Jess said, drying himself with a large pink towel. "He's someone I went to school with a long time ago."

"He looks like a tramp."

"Well, he isn't. He's an entertainer. He's just a little down on his luck." He told her about his old acquaintance, emphasizing how adept he was with his hands. "He can pluck a silver dollar right out of the air."

She was unimpressed. "How long is he going to be here?"

"I don't know. I didn't ask him."

"Jess, you know we've been invited over to the Apples tonight?"

"I know."

"Well then?"

"Well, maybe they'd enjoy some live entertainment this evening."

"Jess, be serious. He's a tramp."

"He isn't, either. He's a friend of mine."

Jess stood in front of the crackling fireplace, his back and legs growing warm as coffee, watching Penny talking with Janice Apple. She was laughing, her lank butterscotch hair spilling into her eyes. She'd die, he thought, if she knew Penny was someone off the street. She was forever going on about the decline of downtown, about all the pathetic street people who congregated there at night, admitting she was afraid to go down there after dark anymore. Jess smiled to himself, half listening to the desultory conversation around him. Penny scarcely bore any resemblance to the man he had seen last night at the march. He had combed his chaotic hair, shaved off his whiskers, put on a clean shirt and jacket that Jess had found for him in the cedar chest. He blended in easily with the Apples and all their guests, and Jess was pleased. At last he felt as if he had made up a little for slighting his old friend last night. Penny looked as respectable as anyone there.

Setting his drink down, Jess wandered toward the bar and picked up three paring knives. He stared a moment at Penny, then suddenly shouted his name and tossed the knives at him. Gasps burst through the room. Penny deftly caught the knives, whirled them above his head, and began juggling them to the delight of everyone. Jess, grinning, applauded him along with the other guests, feeling almost a part of the performance since he had thrown him the knives. It was his idea not to tell anyone that Penny was a juggler, but instead to surprise them by throwing the knives at him in the middle of the living room, and for twenty minutes before they came to the Apples they rehearsed their little surprise in the basement together, first with spoons before gradually working their way up to blunt table knives. It had worked exactly as they had planned, startling everyone, and Jess looked on with satisfaction.

The three knives revolved slowly through the air like a silver wand, sometimes passing beneath Penny's arms, sometimes behind his back, weaving him inside a magic circle that he alone could enter.

"Where did you dig him up from?" Max Yardley asked

Jess.

"He's an old chum from grammar school. I just ran into him the other night."

"He's damn clever."

Nodding, Jess stepped over to the bar to mix himself another drink when all of a sudden the knives clattered to the floor, and he spun around to see Penny glowering at Agnes Wicks who was sitting on the piano bench.

"What're you staring at, lady?" Penny demanded acidly.

"Pardon me?" she said.

"You think I haven't grown up, don't you, lady? You think I'm still a child?"

She seemed flustered, nervously coiling her fingers through her hair. "I don't have the faintest idea what you're talking about, sir."

"Lady, I can stare your eyes out."

"What's the problem?" her husband asked, rising from the couch.

Urgently Jess intervened, feigning a broad smile, and wrapped an arm around Penny. "My friend here is just playing another one of his tricks," he lied hurriedly. "He claims he can stare down anyone and is willing to take on all challengers. Eyeball to eyeball."

Penny looked at him in bewilderment.

"All right, friends, who'd like to be the first challenger? To see who blinks first?" Anxiously Jess surveyed the room, searching for someone to accept the challenge and ease the tension Penny had created with his silly accusation.

After a long moment, Henry Apple raised his hand and stepped forward, a little drunk, and sat down across the coffee table from Penny, his chin cupped in his hands, and stared at him intently. Penny glared back, and Henry blinked after just a couple of seconds to the amusement of his guests.

Grady Hanlon then came forward, fixing his eyes in concentration, and Penny dispatched him just as easily. The Shattucks followed him, well known for their ability to set their minds on something and complete it, but they collapsed like matchsticks before Penny's gaze. One challenger after another tried to make him blink without success; his face seemed chiseled in stone like an ancient mask, blank, impassive, remote. Someone then suggested that wagers be placed in order to add some incentive to the contest, and then another round of stare-downs commenced, with everyone seemingly a little more resolute now as dollar bills graced the center of the coffee table. Again, Penny stared at each of them as if he were staring down into a deep well, seeing nothing in front of him but darkness. Grady lasted the longest, staring at Penny for almost three minutes before his eyes winced in pain. A few others pressed for a third chance, and Penny obliged, but their fortunes did not improve.

By the end of the evening Penny had earned thirty-four dollars. He was elated. And Jess even more so, believing he had finally atoned for the way he had treated his old friend the other night by enabling him to have the opportunity to win all that money. He felt as if he were working in tandem with Penny as he watched him stare down all his opponents, and took a special pride in his success. Many of the people at the party regarded him as distant, arrogant, only concerned about himself, and he wished now he could reveal to them some of the sacrifices he had made today on behalf of his old friend who was, as Alma said, really just a tramp off the street. Maybe then they would regard him differently and begin to appreciate his friendship.

"You must be feeling in the chips after tonight," Jess said as they drove back to the house.

"No complaints."

"You stared their eyes out. All of them. Didn't he, Alma?"

Silent, she gazed out the window at the passing cars.

"You blinded them."

Penny beamed. "It was the easiest money I've made in a long time."

Because it was so late Jess insisted that Penny spend the night at their house, despite the angry look he received from Alma, and Penny gladly accepted, admitting he was exhausted from the intense concentration that the staring had required. Jess showed him the guest room, and within minutes he was sound asleep while Jess and Alma argued about him in their bedroom.

Jess awoke early Sunday morning with the sun in his eyes. Thirsty, he tiptoed from the room and went down to the kitchen, where he drank a large glass of grapefruit juice and made some coffee. Stepping into the living room, he was surprised to see Penny standing at the bay window and staring out at the street. "Good morning," he rasped. "I didn't think anyone else would be up this early."

Penny did not answer him but continued to stare out the window.

"What's so interesting out there at this hour in the morning?" he asked curiously.

Penny turned around slowly, rubbing the sand from his eyes. "Nothing. I'm just practicing, is all."

Jess looked at him peculiarly. "Practicing what?"

"My staring."

"Why, for God's sake?"

Penny then confided to him the idea he had had during the night of engaging in a series of staring contests as a way of making his living this winter. After last night, he was convinced he could earn more money staring down people than he could ever earn doing odd jobs. He would be like a prize fighter, he explained, taking on all challengers for money. Jess listened with amusement until it became evident that Penny expected him to arrange the contests. He was to help circulate Penny's name among his friends and invite him along to the parties he went to and any parties he gave at his house so that a small circuit could be established in which, as part of the entertainment, Penny would test his power of concentration against that of the other guests. He promised Jess a share of his earnings.

"I can't do that," Jess said ruefully.

"How come?"

"I just can't," he repeated in exasperation. "Besides, last night was just a diversion, a parlor game. You can't really be serious thinking you could do it night after night."

"I can if I'm invited where a lot of other people are gathered," he said. "After a few drinks some people will try anything."

Jess scratched his chin. "Sorry, Penny, I can't help you."

Penny stared at him fiercely. "You're no different than anyone else, using me until I'm no longer of any use and then treating me like trash."

"Oh, be sensible. I've invited you into my house, introduced you to my friends."

"I don't want your pity. I want your help."

Jess frowned, saying nothing.

"You know I could stare your eyes out, right this minute, if I wanted to," he said ominously. "I could, believe me, I could."

"I think you better be going, Penny."

"I could make you as blind as Samson."

Jess moved away from him, saying, "Please, go."

Moments later through his bedroom window, Jess watched Penny shamble off the porch, his shaggy brown hair blowing wildly in the wind, and cross the street and disappear around the corner. He breathed slowly, relieved. He felt badly that Penny had left in anger, wished they could have separated amicably, but he supposed that was not possible. He knew they really had nothing in common except for a few short years together a long time ago; otherwise they were as different as night from day. They were not friends, they could never be, he reckoned. And he wished now he had never seen him at the march, had never admitted later that he recognized him, although he conceded that last night he had been as happy as he had been in years, watching Penny juggle and perform in front of his friends. He had believed then that he was doing Penny a favor by inviting him to the party, but he recognized now that he had really asked him along for his own sake, wanting to show him off to the others as a way of demonstrating his own generosity and understanding. He was as much the performer last night, he suspected, as Penny. And firmly, deliberately, he promised himself he would forget him just as he had before, and he pressed his fingertips against his temples as though to push him out of his mind forever.

A few nights later, while he was shopping downtown

with Alma, he again had the feeling he was being watched, but this time he refused to turn around and stared straight ahead until the suspicion passed, at least for that night.

Times Square

Jess and Alma Rudyard were scarcely through the door when their host, Ira Frears, playfully chided them for nearly missing the start of the New Year.

Jess, who sold life insurance with Ira, was puzzled by his remark. "What are you talking about, Ira? It's not even nine o'clock yet."

"I'm talking about New York time, chum," he snickered, leading them into the crowded living room where several people were gathered in front of the enormous television set, which was tuned to the coverage of New Year's Eve in Times Square.

Ira's wife, Essie, after greeting them with light pecks on the cheek, quickly handed them each a glass of champagne. "We were afraid you two weren't going to make it in time for the celebration," she said almost breathlessly, her bracelets rattling with excitement.

"I already told them of our concern," Ira said, a smile curling around his round red face.

"Oh."

"Nine more minutes and this year is history."

"Not according to my watch," Alma corrected him after she glanced at her wrist.

He frowned. "All right, Alma, in another three hours and nine minutes if you please."

The Frears had left New York nearly three years ago and they still acted as if they were only visiting here in Portsmouth, so many of their references being to life in the big city. They made Alma think of her immigrant grandfather who, though he had lived in America close to thirty years, still thought of Oslo as his home. The Frears may not have regarded Portsmouth as the end of the world, but sometimes they seemed to think they could see it from here.

"Lord, look at that guy, will you?" Sam Atkins, another salesman, said, pointing to a young man on the screen who was wearing a huge diaper and drinking out of a baby bottle. "He must be freezing out there."

"And what about the patriot to his right?" Ralph Dexter, an actuary, observed. "All he's got on is a pair of red, white, and blue shorts."

Alma pointed at the screen. "There's someone wrapped from head to toe in electrician tape."

Ralph chuckled. "Apparently even mummies come out to greet the New Year."

"Amazing," she sighed.

"New Year's Eve brings out the crazies wherever it is celebrated," Jane, Sam's girlfriend, remarked, her large plum eyes riveted to the screen.

"None are as crazy as they are in Times Square on this evening," Ira insisted. "Believe me. I've spent many a New Year's Eve there."

A brief silence came over the room as the camera slowly drew back to reveal the enormous size of the crowd packed into Times Square.

"How many people do you think are there?" Nancy, Ralph's wife, wondered.

"A couple of hundred thousand, at least," Ira said almost proudly.

Ralph rattled the ice in his drink. "Quite a little gathering all right."

Sam agreed. "That's more folks than we have in most of our cities around here."

"I wouldn't mind celebrating New Year's Eve there sometime," Jane chimed in, smiling at all the people smiling and waving at the camera. "It'd be kind of historic, I think. It'd make you feel you were participating in something really important."

"Too many people for me," Ralph said firmly. "I prefer a little elbow room when I want to kick up my heels on New Year's."

Sam laughed. "I'd like to go once, I guess."

"Not me," Nancy said, puckering her flat, stolid face.

Alma concurred. "Me, neither."

"You mean to tell me that no one here has been to Times Square on New Year's Eve?" Ira asked, scratching his nose. "You really owe it to yourselves to go sometime because it's the greatest street party in the world."

Alma glanced over at Jess, waiting for him to let Ira know that he once celebrated New Year's Eve there, but he was strangely quiet, his eyes glued to the television screen as if searching for someone among the revelers. His eyes were so still, staring so hard and anxiously, that she thought she detected that "red look" again in his eyes.

"Jess, dear?"

He continued to stare at the screen, oblivious of everyone in the room.

"Jess," Ralph said, tapping him on the shoulder. "Your wife is talking to you."

"What?" he said, appearing surprised, as if he had just snapped awake.

"Tell Ira about the time you were in Times Square."

"You were there?" Ira asked, his eyes round as poker chips.

Jess dismissed the occasion with a slight shrug of his right shoulder. "Oh, that was a long time ago," he said. "After the war, after my unit got back from Italy. I got a few days leave during the holidays so, along with everyone else, I gravitated to Times Square on New Year's Eve."

"Am I right or not?" Ira barked. "Isn't it the greatest damn party you've ever been to, chum?"

Jess glanced back at the screen, smiling faintly. "You're right, Ira."

"Oh, look," Jane cried suddenly. "They're getting ready to release the ball."

And then slowly, haltingly, after a long moment, the big white ball began to slide down a long pole from the top of the 25-story building. When it finished its descent the crowd erupted into cheers, balloons rose, tin horns blared, thousands broke out into "Auld Lang Syne."

"A Happy New York New Year," Ira shouted, raising his champagne glass.

His two daughters, dressed in their pajamas and bathrobes, scurried out from the kitchen, each banging a tablespoon on a salad bowl. Ira ran outside after them, blowing a blue kazoo, while the others remained inside the house, waiting for the real midnight hour to strike before they began celebrating the arrival of the New Year.

Almost shyly, Alma glanced over at her husband,

hoping to find him looking at her, but instead he was staring at the celebration in Times Square. Her heart twitched as she recognized that look in his eyes. Back in high school a friend of hers used the expression "red look" to describe the furtive glance between two people who desired one another. Some years ago, before they were married, she had noticed that look whenever he was around a pretty young Australian woman who lived in his apartment house and eventually confronted him about it; he admitted he had slept with the woman. But not since then had she noticed that look directed at anyone but her, until tonight, when he was watching the celebration in Times Square. Remarkably, someone out there in that crowd had reddened his eyes.

A little later in the evening, in a small room behind the kitchen, Alma found Jess admiring the rainy-day photographs of tropical flowers on the walls that were taken by Ira. It was the first time she had been alone with him since they arrived at the party.

"They're lovely, aren't they?" Jess remarked as Alma stood next to him before a photograph of a blue orchid, idly stroking the back of his wrist.

She ignored his observation, thinking again about the "red look" she had spotted in his eyes earlier in the evening. "It sounds crazy, Jess, but for a moment I thought you were trying to stare yourself right into that sea of people milling around in Times Square tonight."

He laughed. "It is crazy, sweetheart. I may have had my share of champagne tonight but I haven't reached the point where I'm hallucinating something like that. Not yet, anyway." He laughed again, sourly.

"I'm serious."

He glared at her. "How can you be serious saying something so preposterous?"

"You looked as if you wanted to be in Times Square more than here, more than anywhere tonight."

He stepped away from the blue orchid, shaking his head, and approached another photograph.

"I was watching you, Jess. I saw that look in your eyes."

"What look?" he snapped.

"The look of someone who wants to be with someone else."

"You're the one who's hallucinating tonight, Alma. Not me."

"Who were you with when you were in Times Square?" she persisted.

"Only a couple of hundred thousand people, is all," he said, rash with annoyance. "I was there on New Year's Eve, remember?"

"But there was someone there with you, wasn't there?"

He stared at the white orchid, holding his tongue.

"Wasn't there?" she asked again, her voice rising.

He spun around toward her, his eyes flaring. "All right, all right, there was someone I met there," he admitted reluctantly.

"I knew it," she said, wishing she had been wrong.

"But what of it? That was four years ago, for God's sake."

She gritted her teeth. "You looked as if you still wanted to be with her, four years ago or not. That's what."

He started to tell her that was ridiculous but she had already left the room, the scent of her perfume lingering behind her. He slumped against the wall bluntly, as though he had just received a sharp blow in the ribs. Sometimes, he thought, she seemed to know him better than he knew himself. He hated to admit that she was right. He did wish he was celebrating the New Year in Times Square tonight. He didn't even know the name of the solemn young woman he had met there, her thick black hair glittering with bits of feather, she was just someone he happened to be standing next to when the clock struck twelve, and suddenly, tenderly, instinctively, they embraced in the middle of the street. They seemed to hold each other for several minutes, though it was more likely a few seconds, and then she spun away and disappeared into the crowd. When he realized she was gone he also spun around, slightly drunk, and looked for her among all the revelers. For the rest of the night he searched for her, slowly orbiting the teeming Square, thinking he saw her several times, but always he was mistaken.

It was strange he remembered her, stranger still to find himself staring at the television earlier as though he were still trying to locate her, but he suspected he was less interested in that young woman than in simply getting away. He loved his wife but sometimes he just wanted to start all over, experience some excitement in his life again. One of these days he hoped to return to Times Square, maybe find someone he could hold onto again, and disappear with her into the crowd. He was dubious, however, as he pushed himself away from the wall and returned to the living room to celebrate the real New Year.

High Time

They came late one night during the middle of the week, when Alma was at her dance class and the boys were asleep, softly banging the brass knocker on the front door. Thinking it was some solicitor, Jess ignored them, but the knocking persisted so he closed his newspaper and answered the door. He was startled to find on his porch, at this time of night, three of his neighbors smiling like schoolboys. He invited them in but they declined, saying they could stay only a few minutes.

"Is something the matter?" Jess inquired suspiciously.

"Oh, no," Culley said. "Not at all."

Max exhaled his thin cigar. "Things couldn't be better."

Henry then explained, "We just thought we'd stop by to invite you and your wife to a little gathering at the lake next month that some of us in the neighborhood hold once a year to celebrate Heritage Day."

"Thank you. I'm sure Alma and I will be able to come."

"There's always plenty to drink and enough food to feed an army."

Jess grinned. "It sounds hard to resist."

"However, there is something we'd ask from you," Max added, glancing at the others and exchanging smiles.

"Oh?"

"Because this would be your first time at our gathering, you'd be expected to dig the hole for the pole we put up to commemorate our heritage."

"You mean like for a flagpole or something?"

Max said, "A little larger than that, Jess."

"About four feet deep and three feet round," Culley said.

Jess' eyes rounded in amazement at the dimensions of the hole.

Henry noted then that, a few years ago when the state was celebrating its centennial, a schoolteacher who was then residing in the neighborhood came across an article in her reading about how the early settlers sometimes used to keep special trees on high ground that in cases of emergency they would set on fire to signal their neighbors for help, and she suggested the neighborhood might do its part in celebrating the centennial by erecting what she referred to as their own Heritage pole. And so they did, finding a large cedar tree that they stripped and decorated and signed with their initials, and ever since then the practice had continued, with a different person tapped each year to plant the pole. He claimed it was regarded among most of the neighbors as quite an honor to be selected as a digger.

"You make it sound like climbing a mountain," Jess said.

"It's definitely an ordeal all right that requires a lot of plain old hard work," Henry said. "But I'm sure it provides as much satisfaction as anyone climbing a mountain could hope to experience."

"Has anybody ever refused?" Jess asked.

"Oh, a couple have," Max said edgily. "Klein, a chemist who lives a couple of blocks from here, and someone else whose name escapes me. Just the sort of folks you'd expected to refuse really . . . the kind who never whistle any tune but their own."

"So, Jess, will you do it?" Henry asked.

Jess nodded. "I guess."

"Don't look so glum, my man," he advised. "You'll have the time of your life up there. Think of it, you'll be doing just what the first settlers did over a hundred years ago."

Jess smiled lamely while the others beamed.

Later that evening, after Alma had returned from her class and was soaking upstairs in her bath, Jess sat in his study and considered for the eleventh time how foolish he probably had been to have agreed to dig the hole when he scarcely did any work with his hands, except occasionally splitting some kindling when he went over to his mother's on Sundays. He sat in an insurance office all day, shuffling papers, he found it straining just to cut the lawn twice a month. Then again, he assumed he was not really any different from most of the men in the neighborhood, who also were confined to desks all day and seldom found the opportunity to engage in any strenuous physical exercise. They were just as weak and short of breath as he was, just as out of shape, which he supposed was why they displayed such pride in digging a hole in the ground. He wondered to himself then, slowly swirling the ice cubes in his glass, if any of them ever felt any of the misgivings about what they did every day for a living that he felt at times. For as long as he could remember he had wanted to become an architect, eventually submitted samples of his finest drawings to half a dozen architectural schools, but had been denied admission to each school. He suspected others in the neighborhood had similar disappointments, and slowly he now began to comprehend some of the appeal of digging the hole, which maybe for a few moments compensated the diggers for the dull, tedious careers they were now pursuing and the disappointments they had suffered. Perhaps, he thought, he could experience that same sense of accomplishment, perhaps digging the hole would be worth it after all.

He smiled to himself, wondering if the whiskey had twisted this odd idea into his head.

"Sally tells me we've been invited to a picnic later this month," Alma remarked casually as she stepped into her skirt.

Jess, his eyes drowsy, remained on the edge of the bed, staring down at the floor. "Yes, we were."

"Are we going?"

"I suppose so."

"How come you never mentioned anything about it to me then?"

"I forgot."

"You forgot, or you were too embarrassed to tell me?"

He looked up from the floor. Her eyes were narrowed in anger, bright as the cracks in the ceiling.

"Apparently, you've agreed to dig some hole for a flag or something all by yourself."

"The Heritage pole."

"Whatever," she fumed. "What do you think you're doing? You've never done any physical work in your life. It's an event just to get you to clean the eaves. You're not some ditch digger. You'll hurt yourself if you try, maybe rupture something."

He frowned. "They asked me, I agreed, and that's that."

"That's your problem, Jess. You can't say no to anyone outside this house. You're so afraid you'll offend someone. That they won't speak to you anymore if you don't do what they ask. You've got to get some backbone, Jess, or you're just going to collapse someday."

He started to answer her when she abruptly cut him off, snapping, "Let's drop it, all right."

"But I never picked it up."

She stalked out of the bedroom. Slowly Jess stood, stepped over to the dresser, and counted the loose change beside his car keys. He heard her waking the boys upstairs, their lame protests, her crisp, firm commands. He removed his pajama top, and before shaving he stared at himself in the cloudy mirror. His arms were thinner than he remembered them being, like curtain rods, he thought, his chest sagged, his skin seemed pale as china. He looked down at his hands, tried to imagine them tearing the telephone directory into halves, doubted if they could snap a pencil. He stooped over as if he were going to plant a shovel through the floor, looking at his shoulders and spine. He was in no condition to dig the hole. He had known this all along yet still he had agreed to dig it because, as Alma said, he was too timid to refuse. Throughout his life he had generally done whatever people asked of him, following their directions as if they were his own. Sometimes he felt as if he were confined to a wheelchair, forever being pushed behind by others.

He sat back down on the bed a moment, gazing at the photograph of Alma on the nightstand. They had been married a little over eleven years, expected to remain together the rest of their lives, growing older, watching their sons mature into men, into larger shadows of themselves. And they had come to know one another better than they would ever know anyone else, including their children. Even so, he wished this morning she had been wrong, wished he had accepted the challenge of his neighbors out of strength and not weakness. But he knew she was right, she always was about him; she knew him better than he knew himself—at least, better than he wanted to know himself at times.

Deep in a corner of the backyard, behind the garage, was a shaded patch of ground cluttered with paint cans and jars and odd scraps of wood. One night, after dinner, Jess moved all the debris into the garage, took out a shovel, and began to dig a few minutes in the damp ground. He worked slowly, diligently, turning over a small circle of the dark soil, digging a hole large enough to hold a medicine ball. Then he filled it up and bent over the shovel in exhaustion, his forehead damp with sweat. When he woke the next morning his spine ached, and he could barely crawl out of bed. Alma ridiculed him, insisted he quit before he injured himself seriously. A few days later, he returned to the backyard and dug another hole, though not as deep as the previous one. He went out every night that week, despite the pain in his back, digging for up to half an hour. One evening Tobie, his youngest son, followed him outside with his small sand pail and shovel and began digging beside him until Alma saw what he was doing and demanded he come into the house.

"Now look what you've done," she railed at Jess.

"What?"

"You've got your son behaving just like you."

"Oh, relax. All I'm doing is digging, for Christ's sake," he swore angrily. "It's not as if I've contaminated him with some malignant disease."

"Isn't it?" she asked coldly. "Maybe he'll grow up to be as frightened and stubborn as you are."

He continued to dig through the following weeks, methodically preparing for Heritage Day. Alma, dismissing him as hopeless, scarcely tried to talk him out of it anymore. He tried to ignore her hostility, though it was difficult, by burying himself that much more deeply in his digging. Gradually the ground behind the garage became pitted with holes. It was soft and loose as sand, hardly providing any resistance to his shovel, so he began to dig in other places in the backyard—around the rhododendrons, along the hedge, in the breezeway, behind the pear tree. On weekends he went over to the playground across the street and dug for a while in the hard red clay in the back of the tennis courts. Over there, more relaxed out of the sight of his wife and sons, he worked for considerably longer than he did in his own backyard, staying at a hole sometimes until he touched bottom, either striking a drainage pipe or the root of a tree, then dug elsewhere.

Slowly he grew stronger, developing the muscles in his arms and shoulders, so that he could scoop up a shovel of ground with hardly a twitch of pain along his spine. Inevitably, with his growing strength, he gained more confidence in himself and grew less apprehensive about the approach of Heritage Day, although occasionally he lapsed into the familiar doubts he had experienced after he first agreed to dig the hole. But then he would consider everything he had achieved over the preceding weeks in preparing for the dig and realize he was not the imbecile he considered himself to be sometimes.

Occasionally some of his neighbors who had already made their digs would stop by while he was practicing to offer their encouragement and share with him some particular nuggets of wisdom they had acquired from their experiences. Cully was especially helpful, coming over on weekends and covering every facet of the ordeal. He even went so far as to describe how the hole should appear after it was dug, suggesting that Jess bring a rake with which to clear the ground surrounding the hole, so that it would be smooth as water. The edges of the hole should be clean, he insisted, not ragged, and all the dirt removed from sight in the wheelbarrow that would be up there.

Jess grinned, scratching his forehead. "You make it sound as if I'm going to carve a statue."

"I don't know about that," he laughed. "But it's something you're going to invest a lot of sweat into and you want it to look as good as possible. Not like some ragged trench."

"But it's only a hole," Jess reminded him, growing skeptical again.

"I know. But you'll be judged by how you've done it, not only that you've done it. That's what folks will remember, believe me. It's a reflection of yourself, like the car you drive, the clothes you wear."

Culley then described how Nate Sheed left the hole after he had finished, his clothing and gear scattered everywhere, the ground rough as coral, the dirt left in a large heap, seeming to confirm the impression many people had of him, that he was lazy and irresponsible, even though he had spent most of the day working himself to the bone.

"I wonder if it's even worth doing."

"It is if you do it well," he said. "You'll be as tired as you've ever been in your life afterward, naturally, but you'll experience a sense of satisfaction you've probably never experienced before."

"The time of my life, is that it?"

"Honest. You've pushed yourself as hard as you can and accomplished what you've set out to do. After that, you're convinced you can do just about anything."

One afternoon Culley drove him over to the park where the Heritage pole was kept, like a Christmas tree, in the middle of a small glade the rest of the year. Jess was astonished at its size; it seemed as tall as a building, towering above them into the clouds. He turned to Culley in disbelief. "Are you sure one person can dig a hole large enough for it to fit into?" he asked. "It looks like it needs a canyon."

Culley smiled. "That's what you're going to have to find out, Jess."

He was more dubious than ever now about the dig. Still, listening to Culley and the others during the past few weeks, he gradually became seduced by the idea of entering their select circle, convinced by what they said—that it would furnish him with a degree of esteem he had scarcely known before. It removed many of his lingering doubts and made him push himself even harder as he practiced alone in the backyard.

Jess hardly slept for more than an hour at a time the night before the dig, despite the half bottle of wine he had consumed at dinner. He was too excited and nervous, afraid he would not live up to the expectations of his neighbors. He imagined all sorts of calamities that could occur, everything from a slipped disc to a collapse of nerve. At a quarter to six, he slipped out of bed quietly, not wanting to disturb Alma, pulled on his jeans and sweatshirt, and tiptoed toward the door. Briefly he glanced back at her, curled to the shape of his ghost on the bed, and wondered if she might change her mind and come out this afternoon to watch him at work. He doubted it. She was just as obstinate as she had accused him of being, hating to give an inch. He continued downstairs, swallowed two cups of black coffee, then drove to the hill.

Just as Culley said, the place where he was to dig the hole was marked off by three orange traffic cones. Pensively he circled the cones, trying to picture in his head the black hole that he anticipated would be there at the end of the day. He grimaced. The notion suddenly seemed preposterous, the drawing of blood from a stone. He bent down to one knee, scooped up a handful of ground, and let it sift between his fingers. It felt as coarse as sandpaper. Henry had told him to pray it would rain sometime during the past week, preferably the night before he was to dig, and he had done so reverently, but the past month had been dry as the desert. The hill was almost bare, with only a single bleak shade tree near the top, and the ground was hard from baking all month in the heat. Carefully he set the blade of his shovel into the center of the cones, planted his left foot on the heel, and began, shoving down with all his strength. He groaned with determination. He felt as if he were pushing through stone, the ground was so much harder than any of the places where he had practiced. Then he heaved the shovelful of brown earth into the wheelbarrow and pressed on, puncturing the silence with his groans. He had the hill all to himself now at this blue hour of the morning, as everyone he had consulted with had advised him to get an early start to avoid digging any longer than he had to in the sweltering afternoon heat. And slowly, methodically, he planted the shovel deep into the ground, feeling strong and resolute.

Within the next hour people began to arrive, about half a dozen men whose responsibility it was to get everything ready for the others who would be coming along later in the morning to celebrate Heritage Day. The sound of their voices mingled with the clatter of their work and gradually carried up the hillside. Culley and Max were the first ones to climb up the hill to see how he was progressing.

"Right in the thick of it," Culley remarked, offering Jess a swallow of whiskey from his pocket flask.

"The ground doesn't seem as hard as it might be at this time of year," Max noted as he assayed a sample of the soil in his hands. "When I dug my hole, I felt I needed a damn drill to get through that first layer, but then it was all right."

"How long you been at it?" Culley asked.

"Just over an hour."

"Doesn't seem like much now, probably," he said, staring down at the shallow cavity. "But it takes a good day's work."

"Tell me about it," Jess sighed.

They smiled and passed the flask around once more, then stepped away, promising him they would be keeping an eye on him throughout the day.

For an instant, watching them walk away, he was

tempted to drop his shovel and follow them down the hillside. He looked almost desperately at the small scratch he had dug so far, contemplating how much work was ahead of him, but resisted the temptation and planted his shovel deep into the ground. Half an hour later, the hole remained little more than a flat depression, a giant's footstep; only after another hour did it begin to develop the dimensions required for the enormous hole he was digging, gradually widening out to the limits of the cones and sinking him down to his calves. Straightening then, he stood back a moment and for the first time that morning he began to feel some pride in what he was doing. The hole was finally growing dark, he thought, smiling. In four hours, he calculated, maybe less if he could maintain the same pace, he would be down to his shoulders in the hole, through at last. He pushed ahead then, feeling almost exhilarated despite the pain in his back, which slowly was spreading up his spine to the back of his neck.

The pain he could ignore, he believed; what increasingly concerned him was the heat. He had never dug in the hot part of the day before, and he was worried about becoming exhausted and collapsing as another digger had a few years ago. Anxiously he swallowed salt tablets every hour and sipped cupfuls of water from the lister bag that hung from the shade tree. He was determined to finish as early as possible before the heat became too oppressive.

"You're not up here to dig your own grave," Henry cautioned after watching him a minute.

"Rest on your oars a bit," Culley advised. "There's no hurry, really."

As the day wore on, more and more people made the

steep walk up the hillside to survey how he was coming along, including some of the wives, who cradled children in their arms and sipped paper cups of beer. Inevitably they would inquire where Alma was, wondering if she lacked confidence in him, and at first he would lie and tell them she was not feeling very well, but then he began to ignore their questions as he became absorbed in finishing the hole. He was slowly falling behind despite how hard he pushed himself, and he became angry when he realized he would have to be out in the heat all afternoon. He began to resent all the people coming up to observe him as if he were nailed to a cross and refused to acknowledge them anymore, including Culley. Increasingly his patience thinned until finally, hearing Henry's wife suggest he should lift the shovel more with his knees than his back, he glared at her and growled, "You whore!" He was startled by his outburst, confronting someone he had never known existed inside himself. Henry, also stunned, suggested he should rest for a while, perhaps stop altogether, but he ignored him and continued to dig.

"Let him bury himself if he likes," Max snarled to Henry.

He was convinced now Alma was right. He had shown weakness and not strength by agreeing to come up here, deferring once again to the desires of others instead of his own desires. He had no particular wish to enter the select circle of diggers, to return to the hill next year and watch someone else dig the hole. Suddenly he regarded everyone below him with contempt for trying to include him in their pathetic circle, to make him believe becoming a digger was a special achievement, when he knew it was only their way of settling for something less but calling it more. He considered for a moment climbing out of the hole and leaving, as some had suggested, but knew he would still be following their wishes then. Instead, he decided to dig deeper than anyone had ever dug before, down to his shoulders, to his neck and head, so that no one could see him the next time they came up the hillside to survey his progress.

Momentarily he rose and stared at all the people below him, his hands on his back, smiled to himself, then bent over the black hole and began to dig, slowly disappearing into the ground.

Side Street

It was morning but dark as night. The heart of downtown was quiet except for the sound of chairs scraping and hammers pounding as tents and stands rose in the middle of the empty streets for the Arcade, an annual festival of the arts in the city. Alma, a volunteer, paced silently on a shadowy corner of Yamhill Street along with half a dozen others, folding a streamer of amber crepe paper around one of the barricades sealing off the street. Her eyes were still lidded with sleep. She had not been up this early in years, since she was a small girl spending the summers with her grandparents on their farm. She seemed out of place among the ragtag group of people on the corner, in her soft flannel slacks and shearling jacket; she almost felt as if she were dreaming she was here. And for an instant she thought if she closed her eyes and opened them again they would disappear like figures in a dream. Then abruptly, impulsively, she closed them, sealing herself in darkness, erasing everyone, convinced it was all in her imagination.

Edging slowly along the barricade, sweeping some paper cups into a cone of litter, she spotted out of the corner of her eye one of the women she wrapped bandages with once a month at the hospital. Her heart stuttered a moment, her forehead became moist. Instinctively she clamped her hand over the yellow badge in her lapel, averted her head, and continued along the barricade sweeping up litter.

She was not surprised. She had expected sooner or later she would recognize someone. Since she started this morning, she had searched the streaming crowds for familiar faces from the neighborhood, from church, from the past, because she wanted to avoid having to explain to them why she was here. And the more she searched the more menacing the crowds became, until she felt as though she could only observe them like a child from behind her fingers.

Absently she watched the digits slip past on her watch, one after the other, like telephone poles from a train window.

"Don't worry. Today will pass. And everyone will be back home."

She looked around at the young volunteer sweeping beside her, smiled, and slid her jacket sleeve over her watch. He was right, she supposed, recalling what their supervisor had said to another volunteer earlier in the morning he had caught watching the clock, "You're here to do time, mister, not watch it." Everyone wearing a yellow badge was working here because they had been sentenced by the court to perform so many hours of community service. She had been convicted of shoplifting last June, though she still found it hard to believe. She had never done anything wrong before, had never even received a speeding citation. Now she was one of a couple hundred offenders mingling among the thousands of lawful visitors to the festival. No one knew of her troubles other than her husband, not even her children; it was her terrible secret. Consequently she had nearly failed to report this morning. She was so alarmed at the thought of being seen by people she knew and having her secret discovered that her husband had to drive her downtown and wait with her until she received her assignment. And while she waited in the desolate parking garage, half listening to the instructions of the supervisor, she resolved to make the future as binding on her as the past by imagining she had already completed it, so that she had no choice but to fulfill her obligation.

Up and down the street, vendors at the food stalls peddled their delicacies: "Beef teriyaki!... Escargots!... Chinook salmon fresh from the stream—improve your intelligence with brain food!" The mall had turned into an international food bazaar. Paper cups and plates covered the ground. Her primary responsibility was to keep her area clear as ice water, according to the supervisor, so docilely she moved up and down the street, sweeping the litter into a heavy canvas sack slung over her shoulder. Once before she had worked as a volunteer at the festival, serving biscuits and spiced cinnamon tea at the booth sponsored by the Friends of Chamber Music to raise money for their Christmas dance. The booth was an old rowboat supported on two large rubber wheels, which they pushed from corner to corner, referring to it as the "Sale Boat." It had been at least a year since she had attended a meeting of the organization. She wondered if she had been struck from the membership list. Probably. Like so many other things, lately, she found it difficult to remember if she had left or been removed. Either way she felt left out.

"Cheer up, honey. Don't look so glum."

She straightened up with some difficulty, holding her spine, and accepted a swallow of Nescafe from one of the other volunteers, a gangling Mexican woman with huge loop earrings and a broad halo of hair. She sat down on the curb beside her a moment, sipping the strong coffee.

"You done much sweeping before?"

"Only around the house."

The woman stared at her swollen hands. "Not me, honey. I don't have no place. I like to stay in motel rooms, let the maids do the cleaning up." Suddenly, exaggeratedly, she began to cough until tears slid down her cheeks. She explained she suffered from some respiratory ailment, recalled how she was told once to go to the mountains for the clean air, but instead, every day for a month, she rode the elevator to the top floor of the Hilton and breathed the air up there.

Alma grinned.

"Well, I guess things could be worse."

Skeptically Alma sighed, massaging her shoulders.

"We could be talking to one another from behind bars. I don't know about you, honey, but I'd rather sweep than go to jail."

"Ain't that the truth," another volunteer chimed in, shouldering his broom. "Also, I suppose, it gives you a feeling of having done something worthwhile for a change."

As she listened to them talk about their convictions, the woman for prostitution, the young man for having a few grams of hashish in his possession, she again was convinced it was all a bad dream that she would be waking up from at any moment.

Everyone took their turn standing watch for an hour at the barricade, making sure no cars turned down the street, and as she stood, concealed behind violet sunglasses, she stared anxiously at the swarming crowds, still apprehensive she might be recognized at any second. For a while she watched some office girls browse from booth to booth, sifting through all the different objects on sale and purchasing little; she was reminded of herself when she worked downtown before she was married and would spend her lunch hour browsing through the shops. She had enjoyed those two years very much, despite the tedium of being a file clerk. Often in the summertime, she and another girl would wear swimsuits beneath their dresses and walk down to the riverbank at lunch, remove their dresses, and lie in the cool grass for half an hour. By the middle of the summer they would be dark as Africans. She was so carefree and independent then, accountable to no one but herself, able to do as she pleased. She smiled to herself a moment as she recalled the afternoon she went to the riverbank with one of the young men from the office, who was so shy she had to take his hand in hers and slide it between her thighs, gently, slowly, probing herself. The memory made her blush, as she could hardly imagine ever having been so daring; it seemed as improbable to her now as being a shoplifter.

"Everyone is doing fine. Keep it up and none of you will be in court again."

The supervisor, an officious young man in a yellow corduroy jacket with patched elbows, strolled along the street, surveying their work. After a moment, waving a rolled festival program, he pointed out to Alma some plastic spoons that had been neglected along the curbing. Then, to no one in particular, he said as if by rote, "Sometimes I am asked what does anyone learn from picking up paper at an art festival. And I answer, what do they get out of going to jail? Nothing. And here, at least, they have a chance to contribute something back to the community because if these barricades weren't manned and the streets kept clean there would be no festival. No roses, right, without thorns."

Grinning, he drew on his thin cigar, exhaling a cloud of smoke.

Although it continued to seem unreal, ridiculous, some shuddering dare taken in a dark corner of her imagination, she could recall every detail of what occurred that afternoon in the dress shop when she had been arrested for shoplifting. But for a long while she remained suspicious, knowing how difficult it is sometimes to distinguish what happened from what might have happened, and yet after she appeared in court she realized what she remembered was what happened. Clearly she had not intended to take the two sweaters she put inside her shoulder bag. And from the moment she was caught she insisted it had been a terrible mistake. She had simply forgotten about them being there when she walked out of the shop, having intended to pay for them all the time. No one believed her story, not even her. To this day, though, she was not sure why she put the sweaters into her bag. She did not want them really, she had drawers full of sweaters, and even if she did she had enough money in her purse to purchase them. It remained a riddle that she suspected she would never resolve.

Tired, the tendons at the backs of her thighs stiffening, she relaxed a moment and swallowed a small packet of sugar for energy. Suddenly standing there at one of the craft stands and glancing in her direction was Mrs. Ragsdale, an old acquaintance from the parish, and hurriedly she looked away and resumed sweeping, praying she had not been spotted.

"Alma!"

She continued to sweep, her heart pounding.

"Alma, dear, how are you?"

"All right," she said, concealing the yellow badge with her scarf.

"For a moment, I hardly recognized you all bent over that broom. You look like one of those Russian street sweepers."

"But only half as strong."

Mrs. Ragsdale smiled. "You should have volunteered for something less strenuous. Pouring tea, maybe. Isn't that what you did once before here?"

"A couple of years ago, yes."

"Then why, may I ask, are you sweeping the street?"

She shrugged. "To keep it clean."

They talked a moment about the growth of the festival over the last few years, Alma wondering all the while if Mrs. Ragsdale knew why she was really here. She assumed that if she did she would be too polite to say anything. She resolved then to be more cautious from now on, not wanting to go through the humiliation of being cornered again and having to feint and dissemble in order to keep her secret.

Ever since her arrest she had consciously avoided thinking about what had happened in the dress shop, as though by not thinking about it she could sweep it away like something in the street. But now she could think of little else. Seemingly, as one of the other volunteers suggested, they were expected to reflect on what they had done while they worked. It was part of their penance. Sometimes she felt, in the back of her mind, as if she were in church, bent over clasped hands instead of pushing a broom. She considered all sorts of motives, including the ones that had been raised in court, but nothing seemed conclusive. For a while she had wondered if it was in her blood, remembering how her mother sometimes in her bitterness railed that life was a theft and it was only a question of who reached out the farthest. Yet she had been so appalled watching her mother taking things when they went shopping at the market and in department stores that she had become fiercely honest herself, often embarrassing others with her unwillingness to lie or cheat. She was not like her mother, not in this instance anyway. Eventually, in frustration, she asked one of the volunteers convicted of shoplifting why she had done it, and she said it was only natural for a person to want more and more is never enough. Throughout the afternoon she surveyed some of the others, trying to find out why they had committed their crimes, and discovered that many of them were, surprisingly, as unsure as she was.

She was a small girl when her father went to work one morning and never returned. Her mother became frantic, searched everywhere for him until she realized he was not going to come back. And she remembered, at the end of the week, how her mother swept his room bare and burned all the photographs she had of him in the house. She wanted to remove every trace of his memory. There were a few possessions he had left behind in his desk that would not burn, mainly the collection of whale teeth on which in his spare time he had etched intricate scenes of nautical life, often adding a drop of his own blood to the ink, and she told Alma to bury them outside in the garden.

"They're old bones," she remembered telling her mother. "They can't grow."

"I know," she answered. "We have to forget about them, about everything associated with your father."

She was convinced it did little good to brood on the past and preferred to forget whatever troubled her, including her husband, about whom she seldom uttered another remark in the presence of her daughter. And so Alma dug a hole among the azaleas, carefully set the possessions into it, and methodically covered it up, wondering if she could ever bury them as deeply in her memory.

Jess, her husband, reflected the attitude of her mother. Although he was deeply upset and disappointed with her when he first learned about what had happened, considering it a shadow on the whole family, he eventually joined in her silence, even encouraged her to disregard it as if it had never happened. She was grateful at first, desperately wanting to keep it quiet, but later when she tried to discuss it with him, he refused to listen and cautioned her to put it in the back of her mind, making her recall the objects she had buried in the garden as a little girl. It was an accident, he believed, and he was uninterested in trying to search for an explanation, convinced that accidents are just going to happen. Driving her down this morning, she realized, he might as well have been driving her to the supermarket, for he continued to keep silent, refusing to mention a word about why she was going to work at the festival, not even while he waited with her in the parking garage with the other volunteers. Instead, he talked about the promise of rain later that evening.

"You're getting there," the Mexican woman told her.

"Getting where?"

"Where I am," she grinned, opening her hands and revealing her blisters.

Alma grinned back, tiredly, glancing at the swellings on her own hands. The work was strenuous certainly, her back ached, her shoulders throbbed, but still the most difficult part was to avoid being recognized. Her nerves were ragged from searching the crowds for people she knew, forever expecting someone to tap her on the shoulder in recognition. She was positive it would happen any instant. For one tense minute, late in the afternoon, one of the mimes circulating the festival suddenly appeared at her elbow, pushing an imaginary broom, which drew the attention of several people. She cringed as she became the public spectacle she had dreaded becoming all day and paused, as did the mime, emulating her embarrassment by trembling violently, and the crowd laughed. Then, trying to ignore him, she resumed her work, and the mime preceded her, bouncing from side to side as if he were a scrap of paper she was sweeping, until she reached the edge of the curbing and he spilled head over heels as if she had swept him into the street. The crowd laughed again and he leaped up, removed his bowler, and bowed exaggeratedly.

She watched him wander back down the street and hand a phantom bouquet of flowers to an attractive office girl. She envied him his disguise; he could be anyone underneath, a boy, a woman, a monster, anonymous as a shadow.

If, at times, she felt everyone at the festival was watching her as she swept, at home she was practically a ghost. Ever since Jess had suspected her, wrongly, of having an affair with an old boyfriend she still had lunch with occasionally, a distance had evolved between them despite her innocence. She had denied his accusation vehemently, had thought for a while he had believed her, but instead a disturbing silence surrounded the subject that eventually affected the whole fabric of their marriage. She tried to penetrate the silence but he refused to reciprocate, seemingly content to remain at a distance. She seethed inside, argued with him, to no avail. She felt nebulous, without substance, as if he were staring right through her half the time. Perhaps, she thought to herself, if she was not like her mother, she was like her grandmother, a cunning, independent woman who often feigned illnesses to gain the attention of her children. Perhaps she had taken the sweaters because she was too young to be seriously ill. It seemed as plausible as any of the explanations discussed in court but she did not know, not for sure.

At dusk, exhausted, she collapsed on the curbing next to the Mexican woman, their brooms spread across their laps, and stared numbly at the empty booths. The festival was over but the streets were covered with trash. She breathed deeply, holding and massaging her sore bones, oblivious to the stares of anyone now. She was so tired she seemed on the edge of tears; another step, a cross word, and she was afraid she might begin squalling like an infant. She sat on the curb for several minutes just staring at the street, sipping some Nescafe.

"Get cracking, folks! There's garbage all over the place," the supervisor growled from a passing truck. "And it all has to be cleaned up before you go home. Or you don't go home."

She looked up as the truck slowly careened around the corner, remaining seated on the curbing, then closed her eyes abruptly, impulsively.

Some Time
in the Sun

Jess Rudyard seldom drove his car anywhere but around town, so he was accustomed to reaching his destination in a matter of minutes. Whenever he had to drive a long distance there was often a moment during the ride when he began to suspect that he had become lost because it took him so long to arrive at his destination. And now, as he wound through the mountains, he began to have that suspicion again, anxiously surveying either side of the road for something he recognized, a bridge, a campground, something to assure him he was headed in the right direction. He felt as if he were a blind man reduced to tapping a stick to determine his location. In another mile, a sign appeared, dissolving his anxiety, and he continued on, slowly accelerating.

For a moment, after passing the sign, he glanced at his wife, Alma, asleep for most of the drive, her head leaning against the window. She hardly made a sound as she breathed. He reached out his hand to stroke her arm, then drew it back and returned his attention to the road. It made little difference, he supposed, whether she was awake or asleep, because she would still have been just as quiet. Until this weekend, they had been separated for almost a month, she having asked him to move out, and for quite some time before he left they had only spoken out of necessity or anger. They had become ghosts to one another, haunting separate rooms of their house. Their marriage was unraveling, through no fault of one person or the other, so that Jess reluctantly agreed to the separation. Angry at first, he came to think of it as no more than a leave of absence, convinced they would be back together again. And so they were, if only as partners to a masquerade, when she agreed to accompany him to the beach.

Every summer for the past six years they had spent a week of their vacation at the coast, staying with former neighbors in an enormous old house they leased each August. It was a practice they were unable to break as yet, so they decided to go and behave as if nothing were the matter. They had no desire to spoil the holiday of their hosts, the Stengels, who were the first couple they had become acquainted with when they moved into their neighborhood. Numerous people were invited to the beach house, and when the weather was warm they came in droves, quickly filling up the bedrooms, so that the basement was turned into a sleeping porch strewn with cots and air mattresses. The Stengels loved company, especially Tyler; the more the better, he believed. He was an egotist who relished having guests in his home because there he was indisputably in charge, not under any obligation to please anyone but himself.

The summers there were part retreat, part Christmas, part carnival. Jess smiled to himself as he recalled, as if only yesterday, the first time he and Alma had visited the beach house. Their second night there, they were roused out of bed in the dark of the morning by several figures in white sheets, banging on pots and pans; told they were going to bury some treasure; then led down to the beach where, to their astonishment, they discovered they were the treasure and were buried up to their shoulders in the cold sand. There they remained for half an hour, watching the sun rise out of the sea, before being retrieved like chests full of gold and taken back to the house for a sumptuous breakfast with their captors. It was preposterous, of course, yet the kind of antic behavior they came to expect of Tyler. And fondly Jess recalled other times he and Alma had visited the beach house, hoping this summer they could find the happiness they had shared together in the past. In a sense, besides not wanting to disappoint the Stengels, he had asked his wife to go with him in an attempt to bring about a reconciliation, believing that by pretending everything was all right it might become all right again. It was a gamble he was willing to take, though, because he had nothing left to lose.

As he swerved around a sharp turn he saw a logging truck in the distance with a string of cars trailing behind it, and shortly he was one of those cars, his speed reduced to a crawl.

"Are we there?" Alma asked sleepily, her eyes still closed.

"Almost," he said, as he rolled down his window a little and smelled the crisp salt air. Then he reminisced a moment about being buried in the sand.

"The idiots," she snapped. "It was humiliating."

"You thought it was funny at the time."

"Maybe you thought I did. I didn't, though."

He started to correct her but reconsidered, not wanting to start an argument and ruin his ambitions for the week before it had ever begun, and drove on in silence.

Faye Stengel lay on the deck between the Scalias, also former neighbors of theirs when she and Tyler lived upstate in a trailer court one winter, listening to Dick talk about the solar eclipse that was to occur toward the end of the week. The radio on the railing was playing some Gershwin.

Below them, Lanny, another houseguest, stalked a plastic golf ball across the lawn. He was not a former neighbor but a distant cousin from Faye's branch of the family. He wore a bright floral shirt, canvas shoes, baggy shorts, and a Greek fishing cap. His arms and legs were pale as aspirin, his forehead a light pink. Sweat trickled down his arms and chest, down the sides of his face. He felt so sluggish that he seemed a hostage of the heat, straining just to walk after the ball. He was a very tall man. When he rose up after striking the golf ball, it seemed as if he were going to rise straight into the clouds. Years ago, as a youngster, he had been terribly self-conscious about his height, dreading even to be seen standing up, so that whenever possible he remained seated. Gradually, though, he grew comfortable with his size, almost boastful as he strode the streets like the man on the trapeze, hating to be still. Even now, as he gazed up at the others lying across the deck, gleaming in the sunlight, he could not bear to be idle but always had to be doing something. Anything. And so, intently, methodically, he drove the golf ball back and forth across the lawn with his nine iron.

Lanny never felt very comfortable at the beach, always burned, could not swim a stroke, quickly missed the clatter and excitement of the city. Still, he was something of a fixture here, having brought both of his former wives to meet the Stengels. He had always been something of a loner, which he regretted, so he supposed he could not resist any opportunity to be with someone besides himself. Now divorced again, he had never expected to be here this summer without anyone to bring with him, but the thought of sweltering alone in town, when he knew there would be old friends at the beach, made him come; the odd man out, probably surrounded by couples, but it was preferable to being surrounded by the drab walls of his apartment. He dreaded being alone, being inactive, because then he began to brood, thinking about everything he wanted to forget, just as he was doing this moment, he realized, and quickly he smashed the ball the length of the front yard into the street.

A car horn blared faintly through the still August afternoon, then blared again, sounding emphatic.

Faye stood on the deck, her hand shielding the sun from her eyes. "Someone's coming."

Lanny, cradling his club, turned and watched the crimson Chevrolet wind up the narrow gravel road toward the house, leaving a cloud of dust in its wake. More guests, he presumed gratefully.

"The Rudyards." She waved, smiling, and the Scalias also stood and waved as the car pulled into the driveway, blaring its horn.

Slowly, in the twilight, the white beach stretched into an amber shadow. Faye leaned back on her elbows in the sand and watched a seagull circle the lifeguard tower. "Well, everybody," she said. "It happened."

"What's that?" Alma asked.

"We're all back. Another summer, another night on

the beach."

Dick snickered. "All but your husband," he corrected her, referring to Tyler who had been away all day, ostensibly in town on business.

Faye grinned apologetically. "Tyler is Tyler. He's like a child when he comes down here. You have to keep your eye on him every second or else he disappears. But he'll be here. He never misses a meal."

Dick resumed strumming his guitar. Lanny hummed along with him, trying to compose some lyrics. The others traded gossip and stories, their faces slowly dimming in the darkness, becoming disembodied voices. Talking shadows. They sat cross-legged in a small cove, clustered around a smoking fire, waiting for the clams and corn to finish baking underneath the coals. Jess surveyed the circle. He glanced a moment at Alma, who still seemed to be tired, her head resting against the side of a boulder. He watched Dick peck his wife Margo casually on the neck, the two of them now holding hands like newlyweds, and wondered if he and Alma would ever feel such affection for one another again. He was skeptical, despite his hope that by coming here their love might be rekindled. But even if they only pretended, if they made a charade of their marriage, he would prefer it to being separated again, he thought, recalling all the years his parents had pretended to love one another for the benefit of their children and the church. It was a fraud, of course, but if they had ever separated as he and his sisters at times wished, they might have been worse off without one another. Plainly, it was a risk neither had been willing to take, and one he hoped to avoid too. Before, he had believed it was better to be alone than to be unhappy, but after the past month he had discovered that being alone made him unhappy.

"Ouch!" A shell suddenly nicked Margo on the side of the shoulder.

Dick swiveled around, searching the darkness. "What's the matter?"

"Something hit me."

Tyler? Jess wondered. "Tyler," he said aloud.

Then, after a brief silence, a cluster of seashells showered over them, causing everyone to duck, then a tangled fishnet landed beside the fire, a cracked ceramic seahorse, a license plate, a surfboard fragment, then two black fins which resembled prehistoric feet.

"Hello, folks."

It was Tyler, grinning cryptically through a cracked swim mask. He wore a hooded sweatshirt with patched trousers rolled to his calves, a knife sheathed to his belt, and over his right shoulder hung a torn canvas bag that clanked as he walked. As usual his face was stubbled, Tyler obdurately refusing to shave while he was at the beach. Hurriedly he strode through everyone and dropped the bag in front of the fire, then bent down, the flames gleaming in his mask, and rubbed the chill from his hands. "Dinner ready, Faye?"

"In a minute."

"So how is everyone?"

"Never better," Dick said, passing him a beer. "But you look like some creature out of a Saturday matinee."

"And I feel like one," he sighed, removing the mask. He stretched his muscular arms, gazing down at the debris he had shaken out of the bag. "I've been out finding you presents. Do you like what I brought?" And he laughed hoarsely, sifting through the odd assortment of coins and spoons and bottles and knives.

Inevitably Tyler presided over dinner as if he were back in his automobile agency, talking incessantly about his afternoon, describing the various articles he had collected from the bottom of the lake while snorkeling with some children. He scarcely took a breath, he was so busy talking, so that Faye had to put spoonfuls of his dinner into his mouth to make him eat. He could never conceal a thought, always said whatever was on his mind. He was accustomed to dominating the conversation, seldom interested in the thoughts of anyone but himself, yet no one seemed to mind because they had come to expect him to be the center of attention. It was his house and his summer, and they were here as his guests. What kept his egotism from being regarded as abrasive was the enthusiasm he lent to everything he did. Although in his early sixties, he demonstrated a remarkable exuberance, seemingly regaining his adolescence at the beach. For many of his guests, he was something of an inspiration, someone to lead them out of their numbing routine for a while. "Never the same day twice" was his constant demand of himself and his guests.

"So what's on the agenda for the week?" Lanny asked, a doting follower who, at times, seemed more Tyler than Tyler.

Tyler shrugged. "You have to take each day as it arrives, sport. No plans, no errors."

"There is the eclipse," Margo mentioned casually.

"I know," he said, raising an arm toward the mountain behind them. "Maybe we'll climb up there and get a bird's eye view of the Lord at play."

"We might get lost."

"Lost?" he said, in surprise. "But we'll be together."

It was still dark the next morning when Tyler led the others down to the pier to charter a boat to go fishing. Margo, however, remained at the house, still light-headed from all the rum she had drunk last night. Vaguely she recalled dreaming of someone shaking her in the middle of the night, voices calling her name when she awoke that morning. The bedroom was suffused with sunlight. She rolled out of the glare, stared at the alarm clock, and was astonished to discover it was almost noon. Slowly she got up and slipped on her bathrobe and padded into the living room. It was empty. She remembered then that everyone was gone, she had the house and the rest of the afternoon to herself. Suddenly she considered a score of things she could do but doubted if she had the strength to do anything other than sleep, she felt so lethargic. Later, as she sat on the deck, finishing her scone and coffee, she decided to go for a walk on the beach and went into the bedroom and slipped on her bathing suit.

She walked carefully down the bridle path that led to the beach, the sand crinkling beneath her sandals. Two small boys squatted at the edge of the path, constructing an elaborate sandcastle. They were as brown as Samoans, and suddenly she became aware of how white her complexion was, as white as the sand. She felt embarrassed, wished she had brought along some more clothing to conceal her whiteness, and hurried past them, smiling shyly. The soft sand collapsed around her ankles. She continued to walk straight to the edge of the sea, wanting to disappear from the view of anyone on the beach. There she trudged slowly along the water, as if she were scouring the ground for agates. Her embarrassment at her whiteness gradually diminished the farther away she moved from the crowded beach.

After a few minutes she paused and stared out at the empty sea, half expecting to spot, sliding across the horizon, the fishing boat the others had chartered for the day. Silently, turning away, she reprimanded herself for being too tired to get up in time to join them on the boat. She felt lost out here by herself, left behind like a castaway. Hysterical screams rose from the beach. A boy and a girl raced past her, holding hands, and splashed through the waves. An old man stood in the surf, his pant legs rolled up, fishing. Striped umbrellas bloomed in the sand. Stolidly she stared at the people along the beach as she continued on as if in a trance, simply wanting to keep moving. She felt different from them, all alone, going nowhere. Before, at the beach, she had been just like any of these people, here to relax and enjoy herself, but this summer was different. She had come to try to stop thinking about her father, whom she had agreed with her mother to commit to the state hospital. He had become violent, according to her mother, but after visiting him there she knew it was more a matter of inconvenience than violence, and she cursed herself for agreeing to put him there. Her guilt was a hook buried deep into her conscience. She had left him alone as surely as she was alone now. She tried to accept what had happened and to forget about the past, but she knew he did not belong in the hospital. He was not out of his mind, just nervous and tired. She had hoped coming to the beach would assuage her guilt, and until now it had, but without the distractions of the others it emerged again as intensely as ever, making her shudder with disgust.

Margo felt as if she had just climbed that mountain Tyler had spoken of last night, her ankles were so sore as she reached the remains of the old bandstand, but instead of turning back she proceeded past the stand to the nudist end of the beach. As she approached this stretch of beach, she saw several young people around the age of her daughter lying naked in the sand. Her stomach tightened sharply, as if cinched with rope. She paused for a moment in embarrassment. Then, impulsively, she climbed out of her bathing suit and walked between them, oblivious to their smiles and stares, spread out her towel and lay down with the sun in her eyes. She felt so embarrassed and ashamed, lying there without any clothes. Yet she wanted to humiliate herself, as if to expiate her guilt, and she remained there the rest of the afternoon, burning.

After dinner Tyler sat inside his dusty Oldsmobile, his hand pressed down on the horn until someone got up from the table and appeared at the door. "Let's go," he called.

"Where're we going?" Jess asked.

"Into town."

Everyone, including Margo, who was as bright as an apple, piled into the car and they set out for town. All the windows were rolled down, despite the cool breeze coming off the ocean, and the voices of the women, singing madrigals, carried through the night. Intermittently Tyler accompanied them with short blasts on the horn, laughing raucously.

They turned into the Oar House parking lot. Everyone climbed out, stretching their arms, then slowly wandered down the sidewalk, intending to go as far as the aquarium. They walked past a penny arcade, a taffy shop, a gallery full of seascapes, numerous gift shops. A few of the shops were closed for the evening, their display windows shuttered with thick metal screens, but most kept later hours during the summertime. They passed a souvenir shop with an enormous poster hanging in the window advertising the eclipse. Similar posters hung in other windows, on the sides of buildings and telephone poles.

"You'd think it was something these people had arranged themselves, like a carnival, the way they're all promoting it," Alma remarked snidely.

Faye smiled. "Maybe they did."

"Are you still thinking about making the climb?" Jess asked Tyler.

"You mean, are we," he corrected him, chuckling. "Of course."

At the end of the next block some Indians were selling blankets out of the trunk of their car. Farther on, plaintively, two young men in flaxen ponytails strummed guitars and sang sea shanties, imploring people to drop money into their open guitar cases. The women wandered in and out of the shops while the men continued ahead, talking about the eclipse and watching other people wander up and down the street. Momentarily a woman in a turquoise sweater appeared on the corner, looking forlorn, and crossed the street, carrying a piece of driftwood over her shoulder.

"I think I'm hallucinating," Lanny said abruptly.

Jess stared. "She does look a little like Stephanie," he said to Lanny, referring to his second wife.

"Yes," Tyler acknowledged. "There is a resemblance."

Sadly Lanny looked at the woman as she stepped across the street and vanished into a candle shop. Then he began to complain about being single again, going through some of the problems he had suffered recently. "Single life's like a merry-go-round," he said. "You try all the horses but the ride's the same." It was something he had committed to memory out of a newspaper.

Tyler clamped his ears.

"Hey," Dick cautioned him, "you know the rules."

Lanny nodded and apologized. "Sorry."

They continued to the car and waited for the women in the Oar House bar, sharing a pitcher of beer. Lanny was noticeably quiet, as if to atone for all his complaining earlier, and hardly uttered a word unless spoken to directly. One of the summer rules imposed by Tyler was that nobody was to discuss any of their personal problems, which were to be put aside so long as they were at the beach house. It was a rule he adhered to rigidly and expected his guests to comply with, or else they stopped being his guests. And Lanny especially wanted to remain on good terms with Tyler because he was more of a follower than anyone, forever depending on Tyler for guidance in his own affairs. Without someone to lead he seemingly had nowhere to go. He needed someone to emulate, since he had such small faith in himself. Indeed, at times he considered himself hardly more than a mannequin, assuming the attitudes and habits and opinions of anyone he admired.

"Hey, look," Dick said, swiveling around on his stool. "A swimming party."

A cluster of men and women in old-fashioned bathing tights and caps appeared in the bar, laughing and rattling small tin cups, and roamed across the dance floor like shadows in an aquarium. One swimmer carried a balloon, another an oar. Quickly one of the swimmers appeared beside them, rattling his cup, and asked them to pledge whatever they could afford to help restore the old lighthouse into a maritime museum. He explained that several residents of the community intended to swim across the lake on Saturday in order to stimulate interest in the restoration, and they were asking people to sponsor them by pledging a contribution if they were successful.

"Are you swimming?" Tyler asked the swimmer, who appeared only a few years his junior.

He crossed his fingers. "I'm going to try."

Jess smiled, glancing at the others, suspecting Tyler was considering making the swim himself. A central reason for coming to the beach, seemingly, was to search for opportunities to demonstrate that he was not as old as he appeared, that he could still do whatever he wished. He refused to become passive and sedentary like so many others his age.

"Can anyone enter?"

"I suppose so," the swimmer said, a little surprised, "if they're in good health."

"All right . . . all right," he stammered, with a broad grin, thumping his fist on the counter. "We'll sponsor ourselves." He glanced at the others, who appeared stunned by the suggestion. "At a pledge of one hundred dollars."

Dick immediately expressed his misgivings along with Jess, admitting he had hardly swum more than half a dozen times in the past year, but Tyler ignored him and signed the pledge card.

"This is ridiculous," Jess snorted in disbelief. "I haven't swum any distance in years."

"It's just a stone's throw across the lake," Tyler said. "A child could make it."

"There'll be lots of safety boats out on the water in case anyone has any trouble," the swimmer assured them. "There's nothing to be worried about."

Dick frowned. "I don't know."

"It's for a good cause," Lanny interjected, protected by his incompetence. "Sink or swim."

"For Christ's sake," Tyler barked. "It isn't the English Channel."

Later, after the women arrived, Dick slipped away to have a look at the lake, but it was so dark out he could barely distinguish more than a glimpse of the water. He might as well be underground, he thought, straining to see. Then, in the darkness, he pictured himself struggling across the invisible body of water, left arm, right arm, churning his legs furiously. Alone on the dock he lifted his arms and stroked the chill air strongly, simulating the image he saw a moment earlier of himself swimming through the water. He stroked again and again, crossing the lake in ease.

The afternoon was quiet except for the seagulls that occasionally swooped over the deck. As still as a painting, Faye ruminated to herself. She sat in a canvas sling chair with a slim Simenon collection balanced on her knee and turned a page, inhaling a mentholated cigarette. Alma sat crocheting beside her, and beside Alma dozed Margo in the shade, still recovering from her sunburn. To Faye's right appeared a trawler moving slowly out to sea. She leaned ahead, staring down at the beach at her husband and the other men swimming in the shallows, their dark heads like raisins in the white waves. The last few days, like prizefighters, they had been preparing for the swim on Saturday, running a mile along the beach, swimming in the ocean, doing calisthenics. She squinted, barely able to make them out as they receded into deeper water, but she continued to watch as though from memory.

She had been concerned when she first learned of the pledge to swim across the lake, as none of the men were particularly strong swimmers, but not surprised, for she was accustomed to such antics from Tyler. Anything he was the least apprehensive about trying he attempted, convinced that if you showed fear you were a victim. Ever since she had known him his life seemed dominated by fear, stemming, she assumed, from his childhood, when he nearly died from scarlet fever and was often confined to bed. He did not deliberately try to provoke situations to confront his sense of fear, but if something arose he refused to shy away from it as was his natural inclination. She suspected he came to the beach every summer hoping for such opportunities. It was unusual of him to return to one place for so many years the way he returned to the beach house, because he seldom stayed anywhere for very long before he was ready to leave. Throughout their marriage they had resided in every corner of the state, yet they always spent their summers at the beach house. There he had proved himself, could prove himself again. And though she never cared to be at the beach particularly, preferring to remain in the city, she came to keep a close eye on him, always concerned that he might get into serious difficulty sometime.

A motorbike sputtered down the middle of the road and disappeared behind a sand dune.

Alma sat up, folding her arms. "Can you see them?"

"Just beyond the buoy."

"I can't." She shaded her eyes with the newspaper. "How can you tell?"

Faye grinned. "I've been looking a long time, dear."

Dick nudged Jess on the arm, directing his attention to the burly figure dressed as Neptune, with a life preserver draped around his neck.

"My sentiments exactly," Jess remarked dryly.

Descending the stone path that wound along the lake, they followed Tyler and the others toward the dock, threading slowly through the crush of people. Dick was amazed at the size of the crowd. Until this morning he had assumed only a few hardy spirits would be attempting the swim, but now it seemed as if half the community had turned out for the event. Approaching the dock, he at last saw the lake, broad, green, rippling in the breeze. He had to squint to make out the houses on the other side; they were so far away that they appeared like blades of straw. Some tables were set up behind a banner at the end of the dock, stacked with orange slices and cups of water and towels and jars of Vaseline. A throng of spectators swarmed along the embankment, sidled across the dock, ringed the coffee wagon. An enormous balloon hovered overhead, bright as the moon. Tyler led them past the balloon to the aid station, where they dressed down to their swimming trunks and left Lanny and the women to join the other swimmers assembled in the parking lot behind the dock.

"Is everybody ready?" Tyler asked excitedly as he bounced in place, stretching the muscles in his legs and shoulders.

"As ready as I'll ever be," Dick said tersely.

Jess laughed. "I've got so many butterflies swarming inside of me, I'll probably float across the water."

"Suit yourself," Tyler smiled. "Just so long as you get across."

Shortly a bell clanged, and the swimmers swarmed cheering down the bank and splashed into the frigid lake. Tyler, Jess, and Dick swam together the first few minutes and then Tyler pulled ahead, with Jess just in back of him. Dick steadily fell behind as he groped against the current. He listened to his heavy, clumsy sidestroke, reminded of his grandmother beating a rug on the back porch. He tried to make an adjustment, to soften the noise, but he continued to pound the water as if it were layered with dust. Soon the swimmers were as spread out as the reflections on the lake, only their heads visible above the surface. A short distance away, almost even with him, a shadow of a woman swam effortlessly ahead and he attempted to time his stroke with hers, but she disappeared in an instant. A phantom, he thought. He was astonished at how quickly she had moved past him, as though he were anchored there, and snapped his legs strongly. Another swimmer passed by him just as quickly. Then he relaxed, content to move at his own pace regardless of how long it took him to reach the other side. He swallowed a deep breath, laid his head on the water, and slowly pressed forward. Overhead, a cloud of jagged teeth spread menacingly across the sky.

A quarter of a mile across, he paused and sank his head

beneath the surface, opened his eyes, and peered at the darkness to avoid thinking about the distance that remained. He was not any different than his wife, he thought to himself, floundering in the water like a porpoise. The other night, after she had told him what she had done on the beach, he had almost slapped her across the mouth but resisted, suspecting that was what she wanted him to do—further pain, further humiliation. He had been livid then, considered her foolish and pathetic, yet what he was doing now was hardly any different. For the past eight summers he had come to the beach house, always leaving his daughter with his parents because Tyler found children inconvenient, seeking to escape from himself through the inventiveness of Tyler and the other guests. At the beach he became another person, engaging in activities he had never dreamed of trying, like swimming across a lake. He was as foolish as his wife, even more perhaps, because he deliberately came here to do such things.

A shadow fell ahead of him, turning the water a darker green, and gradually he entered it, also becoming darker. There he paused a moment, breathing easily, letting his arms and legs drift in the current, hidden, he believed, from the other swimmers. He floated calmly and silently through the shadow, the pain in his shoulders subsiding. Moments later, a small speedboat approached him, creating a mild wake, circled once then slowed down, its motor idling. He ignored it, buried in the shadow. Then the blunt clap of an oar burst beside his head, making his shoulders curl in surprise.

"You through, mate?" one of the crew barked through his teeth.

"No!" Dick shouted back, indignant at the suggestion. "You look through."

Slowly Dick began to crawl against the current, his heavy arms feeling like plows in the water. He was determined to finish, however absurd it was, however long it took. He imagined he was trying to grasp something that was just beyond his reach so that he would bring his arms straight over his head. A series of imaginary objects slipped through his head as he swam: a coil of rope, a silk sash, a ring, a blue doorknob. For an instant he actually thought he held something, then realized it was only the weight of his own arms that he held. They seemed cast in lead. Before long he turned and rolled onto his back in exhaustion, staring up at the jagged teeth. His arms spread from his sides as if coming apart. Soon he heard the sound of an outboard motor approaching in his direction. They had spotted him, he feared, and anxiously he rolled over and began to swim, but before he knew it they were clawing him out of the water. He was breathless.

The speedboat slid away obliquely, past a blue channel marker, as another swimmer was spotted in trouble.

One of the crew sighed dully. "If you can't do something, don't, for God's sake."

"They'd drown, they'd learn."

They drew up alongside the struggling swimmer, dropped an inner tube, and began to draw her in slowly.

"Better move over, mate," Dick was told. "You're going to have company." The man grinned exaggeratedly, revealing long jagged teeth like those in the clouds.

A little dazed, Dick rose, the blanket sliding off his shoulders, and as he stared out at the long stretch of sand ahead of him, the finishing line in the distance, he suddenly pitched over the side, splashing back into the water. His stomach burned from the spill. Snatches of voices echoed from the boat as he rose to the surface, gasping, but he ignored them and reached again for the imaginary objects that had eluded him before in the lake.

Dick leaned over the railing of the deck, the ice clattering in his drink, and looked down as another couple arrived at the house and Tyler appeared at the door and pulled them inside like coats from a hanger. The brittle echo of their laughter floated across the lawn and faded into the sea. The beach house, since late that afternoon, swarmed with people—more old neighbors who drove down for the weekend and dozens of swimmers Tyler had invited over after the swim. He was celebrating the crossing. A keg of beer sat in a corner of the basement next to a table covered with crackers and cheese and fruit salad. A stack of Billie Holiday albums dropped repeatedly onto the turntable. Throughout the evening men and women wandered in and out of the house, pouring themselves drinks, dancing in the basement, running back and forth from the beach. After a while, Faye began to refer to the house as a sandbox because of all the sand that was tracked in by the stream of guests. Their shoes scratched wherever they stepped.

Through the sliding glass door Dick watched a cluster of guests gathered around Tyler, who stood in front of the stone fireplace, his arms stroking the air as if he were still in the lake. One of several groups Tyler had regaled this evening with his recollections of the swim, which was why Dick was out on the deck, not wanting to be involved in his spiel as he had been earlier in the evening with Jess.

He still was embarrassed about being hauled out of the water even though he dove back in and finished the swim. He had not told anyone about it and was afraid of being exposed, so he shied away from talking very much about the swim. He squinted at Lanny, silent as a sentinel as he stood listening beside Tyler. No doubt Lanny would have been just as quiet if he had been there, because Tyler relished having an audience. Indeed, Dick suspected he was less interested in having friends than in having listeners.

"You look tired."

Dick swerved around and saw a young woman dressed in an open workshirt over a peach-colored bikini standing at the top of the stairs.

"A little."

"You a swimmer?"

He nodded.

She approached him, her sandals slapping across the deck. "Everybody here seems to have been at the lake."

"Were you out there?"

"In one of the boats, watching," she said. "Did you finish?"

He frowned, confronted with the question he had been expecting and avoiding all evening. "More or less."

"A cousin of mine nearly drowned." She smiled shyly. "They had to pull him out before he sank."

Dick glared at her, realizing she was also laughing at him.

"It's all pretty silly if you want my opinion," she declared.

He shrugged. "I guess that's why people do it."

Still smiling, she nudged up against him, her arm touching his, and carefully lifted his hands to her mouth and sipped from his drink. He could smell the sea in her hair, the perfume behind her ears, and inhaled deeply, suddenly and inexplicably wishing his wife were watching.

Downstairs, someone screamed and the whole house shuddered as people trampled through the rooms, slamming doors, and poured into the street.

"What's happening?" she asked him.

"Something even sillier than swimming across a lake."

Then, taking her arm, he led her downstairs and they followed the crowd onto the beach, where a hysterical woman in a calico dress was going to be buried beside a tent of driftwood. Tyler and Lanny, grinning, held her while three swimmers dug the hole. As Dick watched the burial, he noticed his wife staring at him standing beside the young woman and, impetuously, he leaned over and kissed the woman on the mouth, making his wish come true. It was his way, he supposed, of getting even with Margo for what she did on the beach. He was ashamed, of course, but he was also happy.

"Alma," Jess whispered, touching her on the arm. "Alma."

She groaned. "What is it?"

"Hurry, get up." He handed her her slippers and robe.

"What for?"

"Come on, hurry."

Sleepily she stepped into her slippers and pulled her bathrobe over her nightgown. Then, on tiptoe, not wanting to wake the other guests, Jess led her through the bedroom, through the hallway, and out the front door. It was still very early in the morning, the sky a dark blue shadow.

"What's so almighty important now?" she demanded,

after they stepped onto the porch.

From behind the screen he picked up a wicker hamper and a bottle of white wine. "The sun is rising," he declared, smiling.

"Oh, Jess." She grimaced, realizing that he was still trying to repeat the past, still hoping for a reconciliation. The first summer they spent at the house they rose one morning when it was still dark and sat on the beach and toasted the sunrise with champagne. "This is nonsense."

"Come on," he insisted, draping his windbreaker over her shoulders. "For old times."

On the beach, behind the remains of a small rowboat, they sat down around a picnic cloth and sifted through the leftovers from the party last night. Alma nibbled some smoked salmon, her eyes still laced with sleep. Jess poured the wine; they clinked glasses and leaned back against the rowboat, listening to the sound of the waves breaking on the beach.

Minutes later, Jess pulled out of the hamper three miniature whiskey bottles, also left over from the party. "Remember when we threw all those bottles into the sea, convinced they'd float to Tokyo?" he laughed.

She was silent, not wanting to recall the past.

He stuffed his hand into his back pocket. "Look," he said, revealing in his hand a seashell, a dime, and a silver ribbon. "Do you remember?" he asked again.

She remained silent, puzzled by the odd assortment of objects that seemed to have been pulled out of a child's pocket.

Then, realizing she had no hint of what he was talking about, he became angry. "These were the messages we placed in the bottles," he told her. "The souvenirs we had collected while walking along the beach. You don't remember?"

"Jess, be serious," she replied. "That was ages ago."

"We put each souvenir in a bottle and threw the bottles into the sea."

"Sorry, I don't remember."

"You do but you won't admit it. I know you too well, Alma."

"You don't know me at all." She stood abruptly. "Not at all."

"We've been married almost fourteen years. I ought to know you."

"You only know who I was, not who I am."

"And who are you?"

"Someone else." She pulled his windbreaker from her shoulders. "It's over, Jess, all over. It's about time you understood."

He remained on the beach after she left, stuffing the messages into the miniature bottles, doubting if some fisherman in Japan would understand them any more than his wife. Moreover, he realized that if he had failed to repeat the past, he had disclosed the future: there would be no reconciliation, their life together was finished. Listlessly, later, he stood and threw the bottles as far as he could into the sea.

Throughout Sunday, Tyler tried to convince many of the guests who had come down for the weekend to remain for the eclipse on Thursday, but for one reason or another they had to return home. Lanny and the Rudyards and Scalias still agreed to remain for the rest of the week, even though some of them were reluctant about making the hike up the mountainside.

"What's the sense of going all the way up there when we can stay right here and see the eclipse?" Lanny asked Tyler at dinner that evening.

"The view will be better, more focused up there."

"What view?" he persisted. "Everything will be dark."

"Before it becomes dark."

"We can see everything right here through the window."

Tyler scoffed at the suggestion. "You might as well be watching it on television then."

Late the next morning the men drove into town, Tyler wanting to confer with an old Indian he had spoken with earlier about guiding them to the summit. If there was no logical reason for making the climb, Faye also knew there was no point in trying to dissuade Tyler from going, because he was determined to make every day distinctive at the beach. Surprisingly, the women were more amenable than the men to going, and after Tyler and the others went into town, they rode their bicycles as far as the lighthouse and back, some three miles in all, preparing their legs for the ordeal. Like the men, they became caught up in the strange, puerile ambitions of Tyler, and came to regard the climb in much the same way as their husbands had regarded the swim, as something that, if accomplished, would endow them with a certain pride and sense of importance. For Faye, of course, there was never any doubt about going, she followed Tyler everywhere, but for Margo and Alma the climb somehow seemed to provide an opportunity to gain something new and worthwhile from their stay at the beach. So far they had only found what they had already suspected, that their marriages were collapsing like pyramids of sand.

Meanwhile, the men meandered through half a dozen taverns along the pier before they found the old Indian, Nathan, playing solitaire in a dingy cardroom. Tyler sat down, quickly introduced him to everyone, then asked him if he had decided whether he would be able to take them up the mountain.

He grinned slyly, fingering the string of salmon bones around his creased neck. "Like to, mister."

"Then you are?"

"Like to," he whispered softly, "but can't."

"Afraid we can't keep up with you?" Lanny said curtly.

"Why's that, Nathan?" Tyler asked, ignoring Lanny.

Nathan swiveled around in his chair, revealing a thick bandage around his left ankle. "I stepped where I shouldn't have," he hissed. "I twisted it gettin' outa my truck. I can barely make it across this room, let alone no mountain."

Jess stared. "Looks pretty swollen."

"A pumpkin," Nathan said, swinging it back under the table. "I made a little drawin' here, if you folks still fixin' to go up." He pulled a crinkled sheet of stationery from inside his denim jacket and handed it to Tyler. "All you need to know is there, mister. Just as good as havin' me along."

Tyler studied the map a moment, folded it into his pocket, and said to Nathan, "The ankle hasn't affected your breathing any, has it?"

"Don't know. Haven't tried lately. Want to try me for a pitcher?"

Tyler grinned. "Not me, sport."

"Try what?" Dick inquired.

"Holding your breath." Tyler then explained the breath-holding game that Nathan and others often played together in the different taverns and cardrooms.

"You're quite a bag of wind," Dick chided Lanny. "Why not try on Nathan for a pitcher?"

Tyler concurred. "Do it, sport."

Lanny, puzzled at first, needed little encouragement to pit himself against the old Indian because he was always eager to try anything Tyler proposed. And often Tyler delighted in leading him on, finding him a rich source of amusement.

Nathan collected his cards into a deck, clicked the edges together, shuffled, fanned them across the table, turned one over, and said, without taking a breath, "Deuce."

Lanny likewise drew a card. "Queen."

One after the other they turned over a card, all the time holding their breath. A few customers gathered around the table, watching their faces.

"Six," Nathan said softly, drawing his fifth card.

"Four."

"You're doing fine," Dick told Lanny, despite his flushed face.

Tyler smiled, enjoying himself.

"He looks like he's going to burst," someone said of Lanny, chuckling.

Stolidly Nathan turned over another card, hardly seeming to change his expression. "Jack."

Lanny gritted his teeth. Black spots, large as ornaments, spun through the cardroom. He watched his hand stretch across the cards tentatively before it collapsed with a thud, and then he spilled onto the floor, knocking over his chair. Peals of laughter burst over him sharply and emphatically, splitting his head.

"You popped," Tyler laughed, as Jess and Dick escorted him out the door.

Lanny, ignoring him, leaned over the seawall and slowly, deliberately inhaled the acrid smell of seaweed and iodine, watching the waves break into wild horses against the rocks. He felt like such an imbecile, he almost wished he were on one of them, riding home.

The eclipse was to occur in the middle of the afternoon, a little after two, so they began their ascent shortly after breakfast, having estimated it would take them about four and a half hours to reach the summit. The trail was dusty and rough, narrow as a theater aisle. Tyler led the way, carrying a long alder branch which he used like a staff to maintain his balance and to clear the trail. Behind him followed the women in single file, then the men, everyone chatting and sampling the blueberries that grew along the trail. The sky was clear, the air crisp and moist. The faded sunlight slanted in streaks through the trees. They moved slowly up the trail, conserving their strength, bunched together as if fastened by a rope. Far ahead of them rose the summit, ostensibly as remote as the sun.

"It feels like we're walking into the clouds," Jess remarked to no one in particular.

Gradually the sound of the traffic on the old highway at the base of the mountain diminished beneath them, mingling with the breeze rustling through the trees. For a split instant, Lanny happened to glance down at the highway and quickly saw himself tumbling down the mountain. Just as quickly he looked away, dismissing the image from his mind, concerned that if you are afraid something is going to happen it will happen.

"Over here," Tyler called, waving his staff. Everyone hurriedly gathered around him, staring down at the large tracks along the edge of the trail.

"What is it?" Margo asked anxiously.

"Bear."

A frown wrinkled her forehead. "I didn't think bears came down so low."

"They don't," Alma remarked. "We're the ones out of place."

Carefully Dick adjusted the focus on his camera, aimed, and snapped a picture of the tracks.

They proceeded then, one after the other, with Tyler sweeping the trail with his staff. In slow descent they passed more tracks, a petrified tree, fragrant stands of alder and aspen, a slender waterfall that poured into a deep green pool. Dick noticed, around one bend, a rattlesnake coiled in the shade of a rock and snapped its picture. Around another bend, they happened on an open meadow rampant with wildflowers; following Faye, Margo and Alma decorated their hair with buttercups and daisies, picked small bouquets they tucked inside the straps of their shoulder bags. They were suddenly their daughters and nieces, rash, carefree, making themselves up in front of a mirror.

As the women laughed at one another, Lanny, marveling at their cohesiveness, realized again how glad he was he had come to the beach this summer, despite not having anyone to bring along. For a time, he had almost wished he had never come, not because of being embarrassed by the old Indian, but because of the difficulty he anticipated afterward in returning to his empty apartment. Yet he knew he was right in coming, wished somehow they could remain together even longer. He recalled growing up as an only child and often wishing he had been surrounded by brothers and sisters, sometimes even imagining they existed, and now in a sense they did, if only for the last few days. He seemed to be surrounded by people as close to one another as any family.

Around noontime, they stopped to rest by a shallow trout stream framed by thick Douglas firs. It was as cool there as a November morning. Exhausted, Tyler collapsed on a hollow stump, appearing his age. The others shed their packs and jackets, sat down along the bank, unlaced their shoes, and shared packets of dried fruit and raisins along with some bread and cheese. Dick rinsed his face, then passed around a canteen cup of cold stream water.

"I wonder how long it'll take?" Alma asked Dick, rummaging through her bag and drawing out a disc of smoked glass which she had brought to observe the eclipse through.

"A minute, maybe two."

"That isn't very long."

"Neither is an earthquake."

Jess grunted. "Personally, I still can't see all the fuss about it. I mean, it gets dark every night. So what?"

"Yes, Jess, but this isn't night."

They sat in silence, nibbling their food, and listened to the stream whisper across the stones. A single cloud scudded across the blank sky.

Alma stared up at the mountainside after peering a moment through the smoked glass. "We're not alone."

Tyler sat up with a start. "What do you mean?"

"Up there." She stood and pointed out the solitary figure moving slowly up the trail, a quarter of a mile ahead of them. A dark blue speck, no longer than a cigarette burn, she thought to herself.

"At least we're not the only idiots up here," Jess said, lacing his boots.

"He doesn't appear to be with anyone," Tyler said in amazement, since he seldom went anywhere without being surrounded by relatives and friends.

"I wonder if he can see us," Faye said. Abruptly she stood and waved her arms, and Margo and Alma also began waving theirs, all the women hollering at him as if he were lost on the trail. But he continued on, oblivious to them, their shouts carried away by the wind.

"He must be deaf," Faye said glumly.

"Let him be," Dick suggested. "Maybe he wants to be alone."

"Let him then," Margo said.

They settled back along the bank and watched as he slowly edged his way up the mountain like a fly on a wall and Tyler ridiculed him for being up there alone. Jess declined to watch but he could not dispel the solitary figure from his mind, despite how hard he tried. He seemed buried there, as firmly as a nail. And gradually a chill spread through Jess as if he were up there all alone instead of the climber. Sweat slid down the sides of his arms.

For a while after they resumed the climb the figure remained in sight, but he disappeared once they passed through an intricate stretch of switchbacks. No one paid much attention, however. By then the climb had become more difficult, demanding all their concentration and strength. The higher they went, the more dense the trail. They were becoming weaker, they could feel it, becoming shadows of themselves. The pace slowed measurably, they began to string out, complaining of blisters and exhaustion. The sunlight felt like a starched collar around their necks. They began to pause more often now, scarcely exchanging a word with one another except to complain while they tended their aches and drank from the streams. Tyler continued to lead, urging everyone to keep together, to stay on schedule. Periodically he hollered out encouragement which the women dully repeated, trying to sound urgent. But even he began to tire eventually, his voice losing its strength and conviction. "Come on . . . Come on" was all he seemed able to muster after a while.

For Dick, limping with a sore ankle, it was the swim all over again as he slowly labored up the trail in a daze of determination, trying to finish. The others seemed to move farther and farther away, so that at times when they disappeared around a turn he seemed to be the only person on the trail. Sweating profusely, he suddenly identified, like Jess, with the solitary figure ahead of them.

Approaching a steep escarpment, they left the main trail and followed an obscure fire lane which, according to the map, would shorten the climb by more than a mile. It was dense with nettles and thorns, and they had to break their way through portions of the lane. Angry wasps hummed in the heat. After a while the lane began to veer away from the summit, in the direction of a narrow ridge on the other side of the mountain, and they began to descend. No one said anything at first, accustomed as they were to going wherever Tyler led them. As they continued to descend, Jess began to suspect they were going in the wrong direction, but kept his suspicions to himself, half expecting the lane to turn upward at any moment. He grew concerned they were going to descend all the way down to the highway if they continued along this path. Finally he suggested as much to Tyler, but his apprehensions were dismissed as expected, and they continued downhill.

Eventually some of the others began to wonder if Tyler knew where he was going, Dick especially had lost confidence in him, and even Tyler began to share their concern. On reaching a small clearing, then, they paused to consider whether they should continue on or return to the main trail. Tyler admitted what Jess had feared: they were lost. He was angry and confused, bitterly railed against the old Indian, but he was reluctant about returning to the trail because he did not believe they could reach the summit in time before the eclipse. The others, sitting in a circle massaging their legs, were just as confused, not used to Tyler not having already decided everything.

"Guess what?" Lanny said a few minutes later, peering through his field-glasses. "Our friend is back."

On the right, along the fire lane, the solitary figure emerged from the trees, moving slowly across an open meadow. Quickly the women stood and shouted, frantically circling their arms to gain his attention, but he ignored them as before, continuing toward a steep ridge.

"Come on," Alma said abruptly.

"Where?" Tyler asked.

"Let's follow him. He must know where he's going."

Immediately she surged ahead, followed by Faye and Margo, with the men trailing a few paces behind, grumbling among themselves. She moved hurriedly, crashing through the undergrowth, trying to keep the figure in view. She urged the others to keep up, despite their complaints. For an instant they lost him while moving through a dense thicket, but then he appeared in front of a waterfall, steeped in shadows. He crossed a small clearing, apparently oblivious to their pursuit of him, then moved toward the ridge at the edge of the clearing and stopped, shedding his rucksack.

"Hurry up," Alma urged breathlessly. "He's waiting."

He just stood there with his head inclined, staring down at the ravine, then suddenly reeled sidewise as if struck on the shoulder and spilled off the ledge. The screams of the women echoed across the mountain. Immediately everyone started running, crashing through the long nettles and thorns, and rushed up to the ridge. Carefully they edged their way out on the brittle ground and peered down at the small figure lying on the rocks.

"He jumped," Tyler said coldly, turning away.

"He didn't jump," Alma insisted. "He fell."

"Why else would he come out here?"

"It was an accident. He lost his balance."

Lanny, staring, knew he jumped as surely as he knew anything. People have the accidents they need. Dick, Jess, everyone knew this in their heart.

Then slowly and silently they wound down the trail in a ragged line. They knew there was nothing they could do for the poor man now, but they felt they had to go down and find him and be with him for a moment at least. Dick hesitated, shocked by what had happened, then followed the others, afraid and not wanting to be left alone. Before they reached the rocks it began to grow dark, so they paused beside a small stream and waited there in the lengthening shadows, the women holding hands as the sun disappeared in the darkness. It grew cold and still on the mountainside. They hardly spoke a word to one another, hardly even paid attention to the eclipse, as they thought about themselves and the poor man at the bottom of the ravine. Everyone was appalled by the death, afraid as Dick, incredulous. They had come to the beach for assorted reasons, trying to find what was often not there, leaving sometimes disappointed; only now did they appreciate what they had discovered there each summer— the company of one another. Together they found a certain security, becoming as protective of one another as the members of a family. "There was no Eden but they were close," as Tyler remarked sometimes. Alone, Jess suspected, what happened to the man below them could happen to any of them, but not together.

Burnside

As he drove away, Jess stared into the side mirror and watched his home slowly disappear in the distance. His other car became as small as his thumb, his birch trees thin white slivers. In a few more moments, he thought, the entire neighborhood would vanish as if into an enormous hole. Abruptly he accelerated, eager to make it disappear even faster.

Jess had travelled only a few blocks when he noticed a string of headlights burning in the mirror. Assuming it was a funeral procession, he swung into the inside lane and reduced his speed, instinctively crossing himself. The procession closed on him at a surprising clip, the pale headlights rapidly emerging into a caravan of blue Pontiac convertibles carrying pretty young high school girls in white lace dresses and yellow gloves and, escorting them, grown men in straw hats and ice-cream-colored suits. He smiled, fingering the paper rose in his lapel. It was festival time and throughout June the princesses and their escorts cruised the city in a caravan, attending various functions associated with the Rose Festival.

At the next intersection he watched the convertibles

turn and disappear, and impulsively he turned also to join the caravan. He trailed it down long winding boulevards, through back streets and alleys, meandering across the east side of the city.

When the caravan pulled into the parking lot of a restaurant, he continued on, following the white line of the street. It made little difference to him where he went, since the only reason he was out driving this afternoon was to keep out of his house. He and his wife were not speaking to one another again, which bothered him even more than their quarrelling; he dreaded those silences, the embarrassed stares they exchanged with one another when they found themselves alone in the same room, the alarm in the faces of their children, so that he would just as soon not be at home. Sometimes, feeling as he did now, he thought he might leave and never return, just drive forever, but inevitably he would change his mind and return after a couple of hours. He had only the afternoon to waste today, intending to be back by dinnertime because there would be company tonight, a few of their neighbors were coming over for drinks, and rather than disclose their true feelings, he and Alma would then laugh and converse with one another as if nothing were wrong.

He was driving aimlessly along Burnside, the longest street in the city, when he suddenly thought how he might spend the rest of the afternoon. Other streets represented only a particular segment of the city, but because of its length Burnside reached into every corner, connecting everything together. He had driven along a portion of it almost every day of his adult life, going to work, to the bank and church, just about anywhere, but he had never driven its entire length. Today he would, today he would acquaint himself with all seventeen miles of the street.

He turned the car around in an empty service station and slowly began the drive down Burnside. He felt for an instant like an explorer gliding down a strange, brown river as he stared out the windshield. He drove carefully, past car washes and laundromats and pancake houses, amazed at how much this end of the street had been developed since the last time he had been out here. He could have been driving along a hundred other streets, he thought, staring at the same signs and stores. He and Alma, before they were married, were close friends with another couple who owned a cabin, and often they drove together along this stretch of Burnside to the mountains. Then the east end of the street was almost a wilderness, with one or two service stations, a café, and a small trading post cluttered with tins of food and fishing equipment.

He turned the selector dial on the radio, searching for some Sinatra, while he waited at a red light.

Idly he watched a row of modest frame houses slide past his window, one after another, like immense playing cards. He would hate having to live on a street as busy as Burnside. Alma had an aunt who had lived along here for a few years, and he recalled the times they had been invited there for hamburgers in the backyard, and how they practically had to shout to hear one another because of the noise from the street.

At a bus stop he suddenly noticed a woman in a green silk scarf snap backward, her mouth opened as if she were shouting, and he rolled down his window to listen but a passing truck made too much noise for him to hear. Frowning, he stared at the woman as she closed her mouth and stepped across the street, apparently not in any distress.

He passed the music studio where all his children took piano lessons, a sandstone building with shuttered windows. He passed the home of an old acquaintance from college he had almost forgotten lived there. Once a year he and Alma used to go there along with dozens of other people and drive in a caravan downtown to a football game at the stadium, wrapped in thick surplus blankets and nibbling on limes laced with vodka. He saw a warehouse that had been a rustic dance hall they used to frequent before the war. He saw the secondhand store where Alma bought the brown leather chair they had for so many years in their living room.

Until now he had not realized how much Burnside was associated with their marriage. Fragments of their life together continued to weave past him the farther he drove, the course of their marriage gradually pieced together through memories evoked by different places along the street.

He noticed one of his neighbors, Mr. Coble, standing on a corner and pulled over and asked the old gentleman if he needed a ride.

"I don't want to trouble you, Mr. Rudyard."

"No trouble," Jess said, opening the door.

Carefully he climbed into the car, carrying a torn shopping bag crammed with old cups and plates. "I've been browsing around some basement sales," he explained. "What are you doing so far from home?"

"Driving."

"Where?"

"Nowhere in particular," he said, remarking how surprised he was with the way Burnside had grown over the years.

Mr. Coble was silent a moment. "There's a parking lot a few blocks from here where there used to be an elegant old picture palace."

Jess turned, as if expecting to see the palace again.

"It was a speakeasy during Prohibition."

"Really?"

"I should know, son, I used to play the piano there. But, for one reason or another, it was torn down." He sighed, staring down the street. "That's part of the trouble nowadays: we have destroyed the past and nothing has taken its place."

"Pizza parlors."

He sighed again, smiling, and recalled other places that had been along the street when he was a young man. "Oh, look," he said abruptly, interrupting his recollections, "there's Tadd."

Jess turned and saw his eldest son walking down the sidewalk with a sweater draped over his shoulders. He quickly looked away and pressed his foot down on the accelerator, knowing he would be ignored. Tadd also was not speaking to him, not even pretending to be cordial in front of others.

"I don't think he sees us," Mr. Coble said, waving his arm. "Aren't you going to stop?"

Jess drove Mr. Coble home and considered going home too, but returned to Burnside to complete the drive. Ahead of him there momentarily appeared a small station wagon with a bright yellow bumper sticker that read, "If It's Physical It's Therapy." Smiling, he sped ahead to catch a glimpse of the driver, a pretty redhead with small white feathers hanging from her ears, and as he glanced over at her she nodded and smiled. The station wagon continued for another block before turning off, and he was tempted to follow to see where she was going, but resisted and stayed on course.

A block away, on his left, a bride and groom stood in the doorway of the old Lutheran church where, if Alma had not converted to his faith, they might have been married. They did not appear much older than Tadd, Jess thought, as they rushed down the steps through a shower of rice into a lathered Volkswagen and raced ahead of him down the street. He smiled, remembering himself twenty years earlier driving away from his wedding, a stream of soup cans clattering from his bumper, his hair flecked with rice and rose petals, his mouth frozen in a nervous smile. And now he wanted to drive away again, he thought, this time alone, to the end of Burnside and beyond, perhaps to another city. His marriage was a masquerade, concealing enormous tensions beneath a carapace of cordiality. It had been this way for quite a while. He knew it, Alma knew it, so did the children. Half the time it seemed someone in the house was not speaking to him, resulting in such embarrassing situations as occurred a few minutes ago, when he had to tear past his son because he was afraid of being humiliated by him.

Intently he stared down the crowded street, a young man again, imagining himself driving away with his bride still inside the church.

On the other side of the street, surrounded by patches of shattered glass, two crumpled cars straddled the dividing line with a patrol car. Jess was not surprised, since he often came across accidents while driving to work in the morning. They were seldom very serious, usually just a dented fender or a broken taillight, although one icy morning he remembered seeing an old woman lying on her side with a blue mouth and twisted knees. He shuddered even now, recalling her face; it was the only time he believed he had ever seen anyone dead. As he approached the accident he dreaded to look, but did anyway, and was relieved to see that no one appeared seriously injured.

Singing along with Sinatra, Jess tried not to brood on his situation at home, but the street remained steeped in reminders of his marriage. He passed the park where, when the boys were small, he and Alma used to hide chocolate Easter eggs in the grass for them to find and enjoy. He saw the old Shattuck house where, as newlyweds, they celebrated their first New Year together as man and wife, throwing sparklers from the top of the roof. The street, which he was driving on primarily to take his mind off his marriage, seemed determined to keep him from thinking of anything else, persistently drawing his thoughts back to their early years together, which he often recalled with surprise as if they were the memories of another couple. In frustration he leaned his head out the window, hoping the wind could clear away these nagging thoughts.

In the distance the Burnside Bridge stretched across the river, a pale gray ribbon swarming with traffic. Instead of turning off to drive over another bridge, as he usually did to avoid passing the jewelry store at the other end of the bridge, he continued ahead this afternoon, intent on completing the drive from the beginning of the street to the end. The store belonged to an old flame, a friend of his sister's he had an affair with a few years ago until Alma found out about it and demanded he stop. Since then he had avoided driving over the bridge, not wanting to risk the temptation of stopping and seeing her again. But now, as soon as he was across the bridge, he pulled over and parked and walked into the small corner store as if it were three years earlier. Caroline was behind the counter and waiting on a customer, seeming as pale as ever. He meandered down an aisle, reacquainting himself with the store. He reflected a moment on another future: if they had remained together, he thought to himself, he might very well be the one waiting on the customer this afternoon.

"Well, well," she said slowly, after completing the transaction. "What can I do for you, stranger?"

He smiled shyly, a cigarette smoldering in the corner of his mouth. "How are you, Caroline?"

"A little heavier I suppose," she said. "No one will have to shake the sheets to find me."

"I was driving over the bridge and saw the store and thought I'd stop by."

"And pick up the pieces, Jess?" she snarled. "I'm afraid they've blown away."

He was startled by the bitterness in her voice after all this time. "No, dear, that isn't why I'm here."

She was suspicious. "So why are you here then? What

makes you come now after all these years?"

"I don't know."

"If you don't, who does?"

He shrugged. "I was just driving around, collecting my thoughts, and saw the store. No reason, really."

"I'm married, you know."

"I didn't know."

"Stephen will be back soon, if you'd like to meet him."

He shook his head. "I just dropped by to say hello to you."

She looked at him coldly, intently. "Hello." Then she turned away, wrapping a box of cufflinks in silver paper.

He stepped out of the jewelry store, walked to his car, and continued walking as if in a trance. A bleary woman lay curled against a pawnshop, asleep in the shade of its awning. He was in the dreariest part of the city and seldom ever walked around here alone. Right now, though, he was too occupied with his thoughts to be concerned about what might happen to him down here. He had entered the store expecting to find someone he remembered as being full of affection, and instead he found someone else, a caustic woman bristling with resentment. He supposed he should not have been surprised considering how long it had been since he had seen her, but he was, for it revealed to him how much the feelings of people can change toward one another, even between old flames, even betweeen a husband and wife.

Idly he walked down some of the sour streets, ignoring the approaches of beggars and vagrants, until, hearing some Sinatra, he wandered into a dingy tavern and bought a beer. He sighed in exhaustion, as if he had been out walking down Burnside all afternoon. He was growing older, faster than he realized, he thought to himself. Soon, like his next door neighbor, Miss Laurel, he would be telling people, "I'm not growing old. I already am."

A plump woman with eyes dark as plums approached him, her wrists rattling with thin copper bracelets, and sat down and rested her hand on his knees, complaining about the heat. He looked at her, then at himself in the mirror behind the bar, wondering what Alma and the people they were having over tonight would think if they could see him sitting here beside this woman. Probably that he was not himself, he reckoned. He glanced at his watch. Four-thirty. It was getting late. He still had a few miles to drive before he reached the end of Burnside, so he stood and left after buying the woman a drink.

It felt good to be back inside the car, foolish of him to have left it, he realized as he massaged his sore calves. He switched on the radio, heard only static, and discovered that the antenna had been bent into a loop. "Christ," he barked. "Jesus Christ." Angrily he tore away from the curb, eager to leave this section of Burnside, and accelerated past the bookstores and church missions and grimy rooming houses and tattoo parlors. He drove fast, trying not to look at the scraggly figures along the street. As if he were a child again, walking alone at night, convinced if he didn't look at the shadows nothing would harm him.

"I am going to leave you someday," he threatened Alma the other week after an angry exchange, believing he had to escape their marriage as he had escaped whatever was hiding in the shadows as a boy.

She was dubious.

"I don't see any point in staying around here and fighting with you all the time."

"Neither do I, Jess."

"You don't think I'm serious but I am," he insisted. "One of these days I am going out that door for good."

She grimaced. "You only leave so you can come back, Jess. You'd be an orphan otherwise. You know that as well as I do."

Momentarily traffic was halted as a funeral procession wound through the crosslight, returning from the cemetery near the end of Burnside. Jess crept past, declining to look at the mourners. As he moved uptown into the hills he tried to remember the number of funeral processions he had driven in along here, but there were too many to recall. Members of both sides of his family were buried in these hills.

At the cemetery he turned past the iron gates and drove to the corner where most of his family was buried, parked, and climbed out of the car to pay his respects. He felt obliged too since he seldom came up here except in processions. He walked past the worn headstone of his Irish grandfather, unable to remember the translation of the Gaelic inscription carved beneath his name, past the stone of his grandmother and those of some cousins he had scarcely known. Then he paused at the gray stone of his father, took the paper rose from his lapel, and set it by the stone. He tried to picture him in his mind for a moment, remembering how his father had often declared that a family was the glue that kept everything together. Certainly it was what made his life worth living despite all the hardships he suffered over the years. His father was convinced that the bonds within a family were too important to sever, however frayed they sometimes became. Agreeing with his father, he realized he could never dissolve his marriage, regardless of the many quarrels he had with Alma and his children, because his family was what kept him from wandering around in the car every afternoon. Perhaps he was full of idle threats, as Alma charged, perhaps he was too frightened to leave for good; all he knew for certain was that he did not want to become another stranger in the crowd, without any idea where he was going from one day to the next.

Moments later he returned to the car and, instead of driving the remaining distance of Burnside, he turned around and headed back home.

Part 2
Time Out

Summertime

Tobie walked slowly across the playground, searching for his brother who had been away all night after quarrelling with their father. It was early Saturday morning, and the heat was already sweltering. He walked past the tennis court and swings to the back of the gymnasium. There he found his brother slumped in a corner of the doorway, his head tucked against his knees, seemingly asleep.

"Tadd, you awake?" he whispered.

"Yeah."

"Come on. He's gone out in the car."

Groaning, Tadd stood and stretched his arms a moment, then stepped toward his brother. Together they returned home and had some breakfast. Then, putting the lawnmower in the trunk of the station wagon, they drove over to the sanitarium their grandmother operated out of her house to cut the lawn, as they did every other Saturday. Tadd always dreaded going over there, being around all those sick, elderly people, but this morning he was grateful for the chance to get away from his house for a few more hours.

In the kitchen, boiling some needles on the stove, their grandmother offered them a piece of candy from the large box of assorted chocolates the directors of the Calvary Mortuary gave her for her birthday.

"Every year they send over a nice box of chocolates," she said, grinning. "I suppose on account of all the business I've given them over the years."

The brothers smiled at one another.

"Don't worry. They can afford to give me something. They handle half the Catholic services in the city."

"And they can have them," Tadd snapped.

Her eyes narrowed. "The trouble around here is we pay our men in pennies and they begin to think in pennies. You know, you boys wouldn't do wrong to consider going into that line of work someday. You can make a very comfortable living. Think in dollars, not pennies, like your poor father."

Tobie winked at Tadd. "You'll never have to worry about there being any business, that's for sure."

She smiled. "It's something to think about for the future," she said, walking with them to the door.

Outside, Tadd removed his shirt and began to push the rickety lawnmower across the front of the sanitarium, while Tobie knelt in the shade and clipped around the holly tree. The grass was dry so it was easy to cut this morning. Even so, as he mowed a faint path through the bank, Tadd walked as slowly as a patient, not being in any hurry to return home. He wished the grass came up to their waists so that it would take them the rest of the day to finish the yard. He always felt depressed after quarrelling with his father, always swore to himself it would not happen again, but after a few weeks of silence the quarrelling would resume. He despised himself afterward, regretting the angry words he had exchanged with his father, the torment he had put the rest of the family through, especially Tobie who felt as badly as he did later. Sometimes, long into the night, they would talk together about what had happened, but this morning they had not uttered a word. Tadd understood; he was tired of making promises. He only wished he could assure his brother there would be no more arguing, but he knew there would be so long as he remained at home.

An ice cream wagon rattled past the sanitarium, clanging its bell, and three small boys chased after it on skateboards, waving their arms.

As he watched the boys weave down the street, Tobie, relaxing a moment, recalled the many weekends he and Tadd used to spend at the sanitarium when they were around that age. They had looked forward to coming here then, neither feeling any of the apprehensions they felt now about being around the patients, but regarding them as members of their family, as aunts and uncles. Smiling, he recalled one of their aunts, Miss Agnes, pouring them cold glasses of buttermilk in the morning at breakfast and adding a drop of iodine so they would grow up to be strong. Sometimes, even now, he could still taste the iodine when he drank a glass of milk, though it had been several years since she had passed away at the sanitarium.

Later, as they began cutting in the backyard, one of the patients appeared on the porch with a pitcher of homemade shandy. "Your grandmother thought you might like something cold to drink, boys."

"Thank you," Tobie said, taking the pitcher and glasses from the frail little woman. She bowed, a cigarette drooping from her lower lip, and hobbled back up the porch steps.

They sat down in the shade of the walnut tree their father had planted when he was a small boy and sipped the shandy. It tasted cool, bitter, adult. From the house next door rose the crackle of someone tuning in a radio, then "Ruby Tuesday." They listened in silence. Tobie closed his eyes, the shandy making him sleepy. Tadd, sipping slowly, stretched out his legs, staring at the shreds of clouds drifting across the sky, trying to convince himself last night had never happened except in his dreams.

"I wish it could be this nice all the time," Tobie said, resting on his elbow.

Tadd disagreed. "I'd rather be cold than hot. I feel like I'm melting away."

"Not me. I thrive on heat."

Tadd, silent, glanced over as another patient slowly shuffled from around the side of the sanitarium, watering the roses. She barely crept along, she was so feeble, her legs stiff with rheumatism.

"I'm amazed she can walk at all," Tobie said, also looking at the patient.

"I wonder how old she is."

"As old as God."

Tadd smiled. "She must be close to ninety."

"Do you think she was ever our age?"

He thought a moment. "I doubt it."

"Can you ever imagine being that old?"

"No, never."

"We will, though. One day."

"Not me."

"Sure you will. Everyone grows a little older every time they take a breath."

"But not that old, Tobie."

When they finished cutting the backyard, still not in any hurry to leave, Tadd suggested they thin out the walnut tree. They found two long poles in the garage and, standing on apple boxes on opposite sides of the tree, they shook them against the branches, bringing down a small cloud of walnuts. They did this for several minutes until the ground around them was covered with walnuts. Then, on their hands and knees, they crawled around the tree, gathering the nuts in torn brown sacks.

After a while their grandmother joined them in the backyard, pressing half a dollar in each of their hands for their labor, then asked them to accompany one of her patients around the block as he took his afternoon walk. She explained she was too busy to go with Mr. Butterworth at the moment and she was concerned about him going alone because he was a little unsteady on his feet at times. The boys met the tall, gaunt man in front of the sanitarium and, walking on either side of him, slowly proceeded up the street, listening to him testify to how considerate their grandmother had been to him during his convalescence. They moved as cautiously as the frail little woman they had watched watering the roses in the backyard. They passed a black girl fanning herself on her doorstep, other black children playing prison ball in the middle of the street. Over the years the neighborhood had become increasingly black, the children of the Irish immigrants who had first settled here having moved away after returning home from the war. Outside the sanitarium grounds, the boys always felt like intruders.

"What are you fellas going to do with yourselves later?" Mr. Butterworth asked them as they turned the corner.

Tobie said quickly, "I hope to spend tomorrow on the

river."

"No, son, I mean with your future."

"I don't know yet."

"Me, neither."

Mr. Butterworth cleared his throat. "Oh, well, you still have plenty of time to make up your minds. But don't wait too long or before you know it your time will come and you won't know what to do with it. The summer doesn't last forever."

He recalled then his mother telling him about the time when he was a small child and she and some of her friends scattered different articles from their purses on the living room floor, believing in the old superstition that whichever article he touched first would forecast his future.

"What happened?" Tobie asked.

"I just sat there, I was told later, staring at all of the things on the floor. Like you fellas now, I was biding my time. And I guess I've never given much thought to my future, considering all the jobs I've had in my life. Believe me, fellas, it's better to grab something even if it doesn't last. Who knows? Maybe if I had touched a coin on the floor, I'd've become the president of a bank."

The large rubber raft drifted slowly down the river. Their next door neighbor, Kyle, carefully guided it into the heart of the current, while Tadd and Tobie sat relaxing beside one another in the bow with their oars straddled across their knees. Kyle was their closest friend; they had lived across from one another most of their lives. The raft belonged to his father, and they often went out together on the river on weekends. The shadow of a red-tailed hawk swooped overhead, circling.

Kyle, drawing in his oar, leaned back and lit one of his father's small, rum-soaked cigars and slowly inhaled the smoke, his shaggy hair spilling down his face. "Hey, Tobie."

"What?"

"What do you say? Is this the life?"

Tobie glanced around, smiling. "Strawberry fields, forever."

Tadd, sharing their enthusiasm, smiled broadly, despite the qualms he felt whenever he was out on the river. He supposed he would have been happy anywhere away from home today, even back at the sanitarium. He had stayed out on the playground again last night rather than return home. He felt degraded and ashamed of himself for avoiding his own father, but it was better than quarrelling anymore, he thought, gazing at the calm blue water.

Slowly, coming around a bend in the river, they floated past a narrow stretch of beach crowded with people. Tobie waved his oar at a girl in a pale bikini wading along the shore.

"Oh, look, there's Becky," Kyle said, pointing his hand.

At the edge of the beach, moving very slowly against the current, appeared a small paddle boat shaded by a large striped umbrella. It was a refreshment stand. Becky, a college student, had operated it all summer to help earn money for her tuition. Kyle thought she was the most beautiful girl in the city, Tobie in the world.

"What can I do for you today?" she asked, after they had paddled beside her boat.

"Three beers," Kyle said.

She grinned. "I'll need to see some identification first."

"All right, three oranges then."

She bent down to the ice chest and pulled out three

bottles and tore off the caps.

"Becky?" Tobie asked shyly.

"Yes?"

He hesitated. "You've got the darkest tan of anyone."

"Dark as a Nigerian?" Kyle chided.

"No, not like a Nigerian, numbnuts."

She winked. "Well, thank you, dear." She handed them three straws, her eyes glittering.

They moved on, paddling back into the current. Sweat seeped down their brown chests. It felt like a hundred in the shade, Tadd thought, rinsing his face with a handful of the river.

"Becky's lucky," Kyle said.

Tobie agreed. "I wouldn't mind spending all summer out on the river."

"Maybe we could," Kyle suggested.

"Doing what?"

"I don't know. Nothing, really."

"Be serious, Huck."

They drifted around another bend, passing more people lying along the banks, other rafts and boats. On their right fell a narrow waterfall. The river was calm, clear, smooth as porcelain. They moved slowly, silently, as if down a long winding tunnel. A quarter of a mile ahead, approaching a long sandbar, they beached the raft to take off their clothes and swim a few minutes in the cold water. After sharing a bag of potato chips, they pushed on, moving deeper into the woods to search for some rapids.

Tobie and Kyle, thinking still of Becky, began to consider some different ways they would like to spend the summer if they had the money, competing with one another to see who could come up with the most interesting suggestion. Tadd, hardly listening, stared at the tall fir trees sliding past them, dark as shadows. He thought how alike Tobie and Kyle were in some respects, relaxed, carefree, confident, and how he wished he were more like them at times. He was so tired of himself. Curiously he wondered where all of them would be in ten years, imagined Tobie behind a desk, Kyle teaching school, but was skeptical. He did not really have the slightest inkling where he would be then, let alone anyone else. He could be anywhere, doing anything for all he knew. But then, recalling what Mr. Butterworth said yesterday, he tried to imagine what articles scattered on the floor they might have crawled to as children and touched first: Tobie and Kyle, he believed, would reach for something glittering, a coin perhaps or an agate, hoping to strike it rich, while he suspected he would not reach for anything, being as indecisive as Mr. Butterworth.

"Hey, listen," Kyle said abruptly.

Tadd and Tobie leaned forward a moment and looked at each other, their narrow faces bursting into smiles.

"Rapids."

Gradually the current gained strength, pulling them forward, and as they came out of another bend they saw in the distance a narrow stretch of white water. Immediately they swept their oars back into the river and dug for the first set of rapids, paddling fiercely. The roar of the water dissolved their voices. Shouting, Tadd felt mute. They spun through some small rapids easily and quickly, whirling around a mean boulder. The raft swerved to the left, sinking beneath a spray of water. And suddenly they shuddered ahead, bobbing up and down, waves breaking all around them, until they came to another smooth stretch in the river. They were soaked to the bone, their long hair plastered to their scalps. They pounded one another on the shoulders, finding the short ride exhilarating, and eagerly dug for the next rapid along the right side of the river. They paddled hard some fifty yards, approaching the white water, then drew in their oars and braced themselves. They began to bounce again; gathering speed, they surged ahead and crashed through the angry water. They spun around boulders the size of ovens, pounding the surface. The raft bent, screeched. Tobie screamed in silence, Kyle gripped his seat, and Tadd, trusting, stared straight ahead. Then all of a sudden a huge cracked tree trunk loomed in front of them, straddling a corner of the rapids. Screaming, they smashed into it, capsizing the raft.

Tadd, underwater, looked up and reached for the surface. He was stunned, he was still falling, and suddenly he was afraid he was going to drown. Struggling, he churned his legs furiously and clawed for the surface again, reaching everywhere, as if he were a child surrounded on the floor by assorted objects. He squirmed, desperately trying to push himself up, straining to reach for imaginary agates and coins and keys. Finally he surfaced, gasping, and Tobie caught him by the arm and pulled him onto the overturned raft. For a long moment they held onto one another and caught their breath while the raft surged through the last rapid, through all the articles he imagined floating past them in the river.

Traces of Time

Three birds soared past him so quickly that, for an instant, Tadd Rudyard thought he was falling from the towering elm tree and at once gripped a limb with both hands. A cloud of gnats swarmed above his head. Squinting, he watched the birds disappear into the clouds, relaxed, and continued to pull himself up the tree, whistling softly through his teeth.

As always, every fifteen seconds, he could hear Henry down below counting how long it was taking him to complete the climb. A longtime attendant at the sanitarium operated by Tadd's grandmother, Henry was impossible to ignore, his bellowing voice loud enough for everyone in the place to hear. Whenever Tadd and his younger brother Tobie visited the sanitarium, Henry encouraged them to climb the elm tree in the backyard, insisting that the exercise would strengthen their arms and put some color in their faces and make the girls at their school notice them. "You can't improve the past," he would frequently remind them, "only what comes after it." Eagerly they accepted the challenge despite the concerns of their grandmother, who would watch them from the back porch in her starched white uniform.

"Fourteen minutes and fifteen seconds."

"Thirty seconds."

Tadd, closing his eyes, let go of the ragged limb and dropped the remaining few feet, landing in front of Henry, whose eyes were riveted on his pocket watch.

"You did well, boyo," he congratulated him. "Your best effort yet: fourteen minutes and forty-five seconds, give or take a tick or two."

Thoroughly exhausted, Tadd stretched out his throbbing legs and leaned against the trunk of the elm as Tobie began his ascent. Adamantly he swore to himself that he would never climb the tree again, even though he knew that the next time he visited the sanitarium he would forget how tired and sore he was now and would oblige Henry and climb it one more time. Scarcely giving him a moment to catch his breath, Henry urged the youngster to get up and then handed him his watch and together they counted off the seconds for Tobie.

"Tell me, son, what time is it?" his father suddenly inquired one morning while they were sweeping out the garage.

Tadd stared at the wristwatch that his father held in front of him, struggling to make sense of the Roman numerals on the billiard ball black dial.

"Come on, Tadd," his father persisted. "You know the answer."

He remained silent, not wanting to make a mistake.

"Henry told me he taught you and your brother how to tell time the other day. Isn't that so?"

"I can do the half pasts and the o'clocks but anything more I have trouble with," he explained. "Not Tobie, though, he can tell what time it is anytime."

"So should you," his father told him. "It's a skill anyone who wants to amount to anything must be able to do. Otherwise you won't know when to get up in the morning, when to be at school or work, when to eat, when to go to sleep. It's really not so hard to learn if you make the effort. If you tell the truth, you only have to tell one story, correct? It's the same with telling time. If you can tell the truth, son, you can tell time."

Slowly, in single file, the brothers followed Henry out the back door and down the steep ramp as he pushed Mr. Skerrit in his clackety wheelchair toward the sidewalk. The elderly patient had been confined to a chair for several years, his spine crushed in a fall from his roof, and Henry wheeled him around the neighborhood almost every afternoon if it was not too cold or damp. When the boys came along with them, Henry always cautioned them to keep their eyes peeled, reminded them of the time a car slid on some spilled oil and jumped the curb and would have struck the wheelchair if he had not been paying attention.

Sometimes he scarcely uttered more than a few words as they walked, seemingly absorbed in thought; other times he talked constantly, identifying different trees and flowers along the way, reminiscing about his service in the merchant marine, about different people he had looked after at the sanitarium. This afternoon he was nearly as quiet as Mr. Skerrit, so Tadd and Tobie occupied themselves by searching the busy thoroughfares they passed for out-of-state license plates. It was a game Henry initially suggested they play, and whenever they spotted one he would immediately ask them to identify the state capital.

"Wyoming!" they shouted almost in unison as soon as the green Pontiac swung around the corner.

"I saw it first," Tobie insisted.

"You did not," his brother shot back.

"Did so."

Expectantly they looked up at Henry, waiting for him to ask where its capital was located, but he remained silent so after a pause Tobie proudly declared, "Its capital is Cheyenne."

Half a minute later, Tobie spotted a Delaware plate and started to point it out when Henry suddenly pitched forward, clenching the back of the chair, and stumbled and dropped to one knee. The boys assumed that Henry had caught his toe in a crack in the sidewalk and smiled at each other, but when he didn't get up right away they became concerned and looked at Mr. Skerrit, whose eyes crinkled in apprehension.

"Something the matter, Henry?" Mr. Skerrit asked in his soft, nasally voice.

Shaking his head, Henry rose up on an elbow and fumbled with his pocket watch, which had slipped out of his shirt pocket, and held it up to his ear, as if his only concern was the condition of his watch. Tadd did not believe the ruse for a moment, realizing now that something definitely was wrong, but he didn't know what to do and found himself listening to the pocket watch as intently as Henry.

He lay in the lumpy bed with his eyes closed, his head resting against two pillows. Tadd and Tobie scarcely recognized him at first. His long, leathery face was drained of color, almost as pale as his white hair, his lips curved in what appeared to be a faint sneer. They assumed he was asleep and tiptoed into the room and stood at the foot of the bed. On the nightstand his pocket watch ticked, emphatically. Despite all the flowers in the room, it smelled of sickness there, like so many of the rooms in the sanitarium.

He didn't seem aware that anyone was in the room until their grandmother touched him on the shoulder and he opened his eyes and saw them and smiled cryptically. "Hello, fellas."

Greeting him with the box of chocolate-covered mints they had with them, Tadd and Tobie gathered around the bed and answered his customary questions about how they were doing in school. Their grandmother had cautioned them not to stay very long because he tired quickly, so after a few minutes she stepped forward and indicated it was time to leave. But before they did, Henry reminded them to continue to climb the elm tree and pointed to the window on the far wall.

"I'll be watching you," he told them. "And still keeping track of how long it takes you scamps to make it up and down."

"Believe it or not, dears," their grandmother told them one afternoon at the sanitarium, "I was once as shy as you when I was your age. I know I may seem pretty bossy around here, as I keep a close watch on my patients, but as a girl I was scared of my own shadow. So what I did was I started going up to perfect strangers and asking them the time. I couldn't care less what time it was, I had my own watch, but it gave me an excuse to approach a lot of different people. Now I can go up to anyone, anywhere."

Unless he had some important examination to take, Tadd seldom wore a watch to school. And then, since he didn't have one of his own, he borrowed his father's clunky aviator watch, which felt like an alarm clock on his wrist. He continued to struggle to tell time and didn't like to wear a watch because it only reminded him of what an algebra teacher once described as his "painfully slow progress into maturity."

Few boys he knew at school wore watches, regarding them as precious ornaments more suitable for the wrists of girls. One who did, however, was Lanny Sturges, a snaggle-toothed singer in the choir who was three years older than Tadd. Usually he had on a cheap tank watch with a striped nylon band but every now and then he wore a pink gold watch with a sharkskin strap that hung loosely around his wrist. The only time Tadd saw it up close was after choir practice one evening, when another boy urged Lanny to show it to him. Almost routinely the older boy stuck out his spindly wrist, held the watch in place with two fingers, then sprang open the tiny panel at the top of the dial.

"It's a watch you can enjoy watching," he cracked.

Tadd leaned forward and gradually made out the tiny picture of a naked man licking the nipple of a woman whose massive thighs stretched to the margins of the panel.

"Hideous enough for you?"

He turned away in embarrassment, not having seen a picture like that before, yet pretended to smile as though nothing were too hideous for his experienced eyes.

Tadd was sixteen when Henry passed away after a long struggle with emphysema. At the funeral his grandmother surprised him by presenting him with Henry's pocket watch, which she admitted was not worth very much, but she thought he would like it as a reminder of his old friend. And she was right because it immediately became his most cherished possession, even more than the autographed Baltimore Orioles baseball his Uncle Ethan gave him on his twelfth birthday. He kept it in the bottom drawer of his dresser, in a dented tobacco tin, wrapped in black velvet.

For a while he was reluctant to take it out of the drawer, afraid that he might damage it in some way, but then one night on an impulse he decided to wear it to a midwinter dance in the school cafeteria. He thought it might impress some girls there, maybe even make him appear distinctive for a change. Over a pale blue snap-buttoned shirt he pulled on a leather vest in which he tucked the pocket watch, with its chain of hammered gold carefully draped across the front, just as Henry did when he wore a suit.

"You know who you look like, Tadd? Someone who works in a bank," Patty Chalmers chided him as he swung her under his arm in time with the music.

"I do not."

She grinned broadly, tracing a red fingernail along the watch chain. "You certainly do. Is that what you want to do when you grow up, huh, work in a bank?"

He started to tell her he wanted to be like Henry, who knew more things about more things than anyone he knew, but didn't because his name wouldn't mean anything to her.

"That's not for me, mister," she snapped as they spun

155

around a canopy of paper flowers. "I don't intend to be stuck behind some cage smiling at people I don't know. I might as well be in a zoo then."

"Neither do I," he said lamely, not really having any idea what he wanted to do after he got out of high school. If Henry were still around, he believed, he would probably have some advice for him, but he wasn't, so Tadd was without a clue.

Surprising himself after what Patty said to him, Tadd began to carry the watch to school, not on display as he did at the dance but buried deep in a pocket so that not even the chain was visible. He was not sure why he did, though he supposed it was a small way of expressing his appreciation for everything Henry did for him and his brother. It also served as a useful distraction which he would pull out whenever he was bored, in order to practice telling time. Out of his pocket it ticked so loudly that it prompted more than a few classmates to accuse him of bringing a bomb on the premises.

The sergeant in charge of the jail glowered at Tadd when he was brought before his desk. "Give me your belt and the laces from your shoes," he snarled through his tobacco-stained teeth. "And if you've got any valuables with you, I want them too."

"I've got a pocket watch."

He handed him a manila envelope. "Put it in here."

"How come?" he asked nervously.

"Because I said so, friend."

Tadd was then led down a narrow corridor to an empty cell whose apple-green walls were black with inscriptions.

The air was stale and smelled of disinfectant. Somewhere else in the cell block a hoarse voice sang some country song he had heard on the radio but could not identify. Angrily he paced the squalid cell, still finding it difficult to believe he was actually in jail. Out later tonight than he should have been, he was picked up for curfew violation, but instead of receiving a stern warning as he had in the past he was slapped in cuffs and brought here.

After several minutes he plopped down on the wafer-thin bunk and stared blankly at the inscriptions on the walls, waiting for his father to come down to the station house and take him home. Without his pocket watch he didn't know what time it was exactly, but he reckoned if the desk sergeant called right away his father would be here in about twenty minutes. He suspected, however, the sergeant would not call for quite a while because he wanted him to sit in the cell long enough to appreciate what happened to folks who didn't obey the law.

He shuddered at the thought of what it must be like to be here day after day, doing absolutely nothing. A minute was too long, as far as he was concerned, a whole week or more of such idleness unbearable. So, as he waited for his father to come, he began to count silently, One Mississippi, Two Mississippi, Three Mississippi, Four Mississippi...

One day, coming home on the bus, his mother lost the gold chatelaine watch his father bought for her while stationed in England during the war. She reported it missing to the transit company and was informed she would be contacted if it was turned in to the lost and found department, but she never heard a word from anyone there. She was not surprised, sure whoever found her watch kept it because it was quite valuable. It had a loose strap which she had intended for weeks to get fixed without ever getting around to it, so she blamed herself for its loss.

Nearly five and a half months later she received in the mail, in a small clasped envelope, her watch with the strap still loose. Also in the envelope was a folded sheet of lined schoolpaper in which the sender confessed that he had taken the watch off her wrist that afternoon on the bus. Repeatedly he said how sorry he was for what he did, attributing it to all the wine he had been drinking that day. He hoped she saw it in her heart to forgive him and said he would like to apologize to her in person and offered to meet her the following Saturday at noon under the clock at the train station. His name was Arnold, and he said he would be wearing a blue watch cap and a Navy pea jacket.

"Are you going to meet him?" Tadd asked after she showed him the letter.

"I don't think so."

"Why not?"

"I wouldn't know what to say to the man," she admitted. "Besides, I've promised to take your grand-mother to the market on Saturday."

"It might be your only time to meet him, you know."

She sighed. "There's a time in every person's life for some things, I suppose, and I've had more than my share of them. I believe I can miss this one without too much regret."

"You made any decision yet about what you're going to do with yourself after graduation?" Patty asked Tadd as they strolled through the maze of booths at the spring carnival.

He shrugged, nibbling at her cone of cotton candy. "No, not really."

"You better get a move on, fella. It's not that far away, you know. Only two and a half months."

"I know my parents want me to go to college like you," he conceded. "But I've never liked school much, and it's never liked me very much, either. And I can't imagine I'd like college any more than I have high school."

"You won't know until you try it."

Frowning, he abruptly stopped at one of the booths and threw some softballs at a stack of battered milk cans, but didn't win anything more than a green ribbon.

"I've got an idea how you can figure out what to do after you get out of high school," she continued after they left the throw booth.

"I'm almost afraid to ask."

Grinning faintly, she pointed a finger across his left shoulder. "Over there, lazy bones."

He wheeled around and immediately saw the psychic's booth with the faded blue palm emblazoned on its weathered awning. "Oh, right," he laughed. "That's just the place I want to go all right."

"It's a matter of convenience, Tadd. You go in there, you'll find out all you need to know and you won't have to bother about making any decisions."

"Don't be ridiculous."

"Come on," she insisted, seizing his hand. "It can't do you any harm. And you need all the advice you can get."

She drew back the beaded curtain and coaxed him inside the tent, and at a round metal table they were surprised to find, instead of an overweight woman dressed in peasant clothes, a spectacled little man in a brown cardigan sweater with peninsula-shaped sideburns. His hands were laced with blue veins, his chin stubbled. At once he reminded them of their high school principal, Mr. Schwimmer. A crude sign on the table identified him only as Lamar.

"Sit down, please, and give me something so I can get to know you."

Tadd sat at the table while Patty remained by the curtain. "Like what?"

"Something personal," Lamar said. "If you've got a watch, that'll be fine."

He dug into his pocket and set his watch on the flimsy table.

Lamar held the pocket watch in his hand and slowly rubbed it between his whisker-slim fingers. "This time-piece belonged to someone who, if not a relative of yours, was as close as one."

Tadd, silent, was not impressed, figuring the observation was so broad it could apply to almost anyone in possession of an old pocket watch.

"He was someone who did not do something until he was sure the time was right. But when it was right he believed if he stuck at it long enough, it would eventually turn out as he wanted it to."

Tadd remained silent.

Again the man rubbed the pocket watch, his drooping face scrunched in thought. "This person who had the watch before you was someone you admired very much, someone you hope to pattern yourself after someday."

Anxiously he sprang up from the chair and grabbed his pocket watch out of the psychic's hands and stormed out of the tent.

"What'd you do that for?" Patty demanded as she followed him through the beaded curtain.

He frowned, slipping the watch back into his trouser pocket. "I don't need to be told my future, not by some old fool who doesn't know what he's talking about. I'll find it out for myself, thank you."

The oak tree across the street from the lodge hall where his high school class was celebrating their graduation that afternoon was almost the height of the elm at the sanitarium. Thick as a nail keg, it provided enough shade to cover the entire corner of the block. Because it was sweltering inside the old building, Tadd came out for some fresh air after a few minutes and noticed the tree. He stepped into its shade for a moment, then on an impulse pushed up the sleeves of his long blue gown and began to climb it. Around thirty feet he paused in exhaustion, his arms aching, and looked down at all the people gathered in front of the lodge. At that moment he imagined Henry there among them, and despite his fatigue he reached for the next limb and continued up the tree.

Fast Times

The dark maroon getaway car, displayed on a platform in a corner of the fairground, gleamed in the sweltering July heat. Its red wire wheels almost appeared to be on fire in the harsh sunlight.

Quine, the owner of the car, stood with one foot on the running board. He was wearing a hard straw hat similar to the kind worn by a previous owner, the notorious public menace of the thirties, John Dillinger. He also wore an empty shoulder holster under his left arm. Methodically, for the fourth time this afternoon, he described to the dozen people gathered around the platform how, during a bank robbery, Dillinger would often hurdle the teller counter rather than simply walk around it because he was such an enormous fan of Douglas Fairbanks. Then, stepping off the running board, Quine suddenly leaped across the platform as if he were Dillinger, spraying an imaginary machine gun through the air.

Tadd, sucking a blue Popsicle, smiled at the abrupt gesture along with some others in the crowd.

A little out of breath, Quine then pointed out several bullet holes on the right side of the elegant old Essex Terraplane, informing his audience that they came as a result of a chase after a bank robbery in East Chicago, Indiana. He also shook some roofing nails across the platform, which he said was customary for Dillinger and his gang to do whenever they were making a getaway.

Slowly he circled the Terraplane, tracing a finger across the roof. "Dillinger learned sooner than most of us that sometimes we must travel in the direction of our fear," he declared solemnly.

Quine gave his spiel every forty-five minutes, sometimes oftener on the weekend when more people attended the fair. He had given it so many times, he could give it in his sleep, and at moments seemed to be half asleep as he spoke. A seventh grade teacher, he purchased the getaway car three years ago on an impulse, and for the last two summers spent his vacation touring different fairs and carnivals with his historic car. He seldom made any money from the car, considering how much he had to put into it to make it presentable, but he didn't really mind because he enjoyed his link with someone as famous as John Dillinger. It made him seem special, different somehow from all the others at the carnivals and fairs where he appeared.

Tadd hardly ever missed Quine's presentation, for he was as fond of the Terraplane as Quine seemingly was. Trying to earn some pocket money, he looked for odd jobs at the fair and, as soon as he spotted the getaway car, he asked Quine if he needed someone to take care of it. He did, and early every morning Tadd was at the fairground, scrubbing away every speck of dirt and polishing the car until it was immaculate.

As he listened to Quine give his spiel, he always

observed the people clustered around the car, concerned that someone might spill something on it or scratch it by accident. Toward the end of last summer, Quine told him, an inebriated woman got behind the steering wheel before he saw her and gouged the dashboard with one of her mood rings. The coil of rope around the car was small protection against some people, especially late at night.

"You never know when some idiot is going to think he's entitled to make a getaway in my car," he complained to Tadd one evening. "I always have to keep my eyes peeled when I have the car on display."

Tadd didn't have a license to drive, only a learner's permit, but he dreamed of someday driving a car as elegant as the Terraplane. Consequently he was protective of it, knowing if it belonged to him he would be as concerned about its condition as Quine. If an elbow so much as strayed across the rope, he came forward to remind the person not to touch the car. He wanted it to shine fiercely, every inch of it, just like Quine.

At the end of the day Quine returned the car to the flatbed trailer he used to transport it in as he followed the carnival and fair circuit over the course of the summer. Often he invited Tadd to join him in the car, and eagerly the young man hopped into the spacious back seat, and together they drove it onto the trailer. Some evenings, depending on his disposition, Quine drove Tadd around the empty fairground for a few minutes, talking about whatever was on his mind.

Once, after Tadd asked him about some of the other getaway cars used by Dillinger, Quine shrugged his shoulders and admitted his ignorance, saying that all he knew about the infamous gangster was included in his ten-minute talk. "Otherwise I don't know any more than you do, son."

Tadd was surprised. "I'd figured you'd had a long interest in Dillinger."

"No, not at all." He swerved the car around a tent stake, barely missing an overturned waste basket. "About all I ever knew about him before I got this car was that he was a bank robber who reputedly robbed those who had become rich by robbing the poor, and that he was eventually set up by a woman in a red dress and shot dead outside a picture house in Chicago."

"Then how come you have his getaway car?"

"Not because I'm any admirer of him. That's for sure."

"For the money then?"

His bottle green eyes sparkled. "If I were in it for the money, son, I wouldn't be in it."

"So why?"

"I suppose I just liked the idea of having my own getaway car." He pressed his foot down on the accelerator, slowly picking up speed as he began his second circuit of the fairground. "I figured it'd give me something to do in the summer other than lying around in the sun and gaining weight. It'd get me out of the house, if you know what I mean."

"I know."

"Do you, son?"

His eyes were grave. "One of these days I'm going to have my own car, maybe not one as fancy as yours, but my own. And I'm going to get behind the wheel and put it into gear and just take off and never look back."

"And where will you go?"

He stared out the windshield. "I haven't a clue. I just

want to get away."

"Listen, son, there's no point in leaving a place unless you have somewhere to go to, a destination. Trust my gray hairs. Otherwise you'll just be headed nowhere and getting there fast."

Tadd smiled at Quine's apparent concern. "I don't have to worry about destinations yet, sir. It'll be a long time before I have my own car."

"You never know, son."

One night, watching over the Terraplane as Quine delivered his spiel, Tadd suddenly found himself standing beside someone he knew from high school. Rory was a couple of years older than Tadd, but also without a driver's license: it had been suspended for six months because of all the speeding tickets he had accumulated in his father's Oldsmobile. A blue stubble of beard covered his blunt chin.

"You interested in gangsters and G-men, Tadd?"

"Sort of."

He shook his head in agreement. "I wouldn't have minded being around in those times. Back then things were happening. Every day meant something. Every day was history."

Tadd tried to ignore him, hoping he would leave. Rory was an agreeable enough person but someone who always seemed to be getting into trouble. He reminded Tadd of an apple, a shiny green apple that once bitten into would reveal a worm inside.

"Hey, you want to see what else is going on around here?"

"I can't."

"How come?"

"I'm busy here."

"Doing what?"

Tadd explained then how he was responsible for looking after the getaway car, making sure no one in the crowd damaged it.

"Does it run?"

"Yeah."

A cold smile stirred in the corners of his mouth. "I wouldn't mind going for a ride in it."

"You can't," Tadd said emphatically.

"What do you mean, I can't?"

"You heard me."

"This is America, isn't it? I can do any damn thing I please."

Tadd glared at him, his scalp tingling. "This car is an antique. It's worth an awful lot of money."

"I'm not interested in buying it," Rory snapped, stepping back from the coil of rope surrounding the Terraplane. "I just want to go for a ride in it."

"You can't, I told you."

"So you said."

Anxiously he watched Rory move past the milk-bottle booth, gradually merging into the crowded midway. Then he glanced back at Quine, who was near the end of his spiel, wishing to God he had not spoken with Rory tonight. He knew exactly what he had in mind when he said he'd like to go for a ride in the getaway car. He wanted to take it out for a joy ride.

The last time he had been with Rory, almost two months ago now, he was leaving school late one evening when Rory asked him if he wanted a ride home. Rory was with another guy from school, driving a brand new red Fury with all the windows rolled down, the radio blaring the Beach Boys. Tadd accepted the ride, a little surprised to see Rory driving the Fury instead of his father's rusting old Oldsmobile.

"Your family get a new car?"

Smiling faintly, Rory said, "I guess you could say that."

"Christ, tell him, Rory. You took it."

"You stole it?"

"Hey, not to worry. It's a friend of a friend's family car. She won't really mind."

"The hell she won't," his friend barked, snickering.

Gravely Rory stared at his friend, then at Tadd in the back seat. "It doesn't seem fair that it's always the same people who get things that are brand new. I just thought I'd like to have something that's new for a change."

"You can't take something that doesn't belong to you," Tadd protested lamely.

"I don't intend to keep it, friend, just ride around in it for a while. No big deal."

Ever since then, Tadd had kept his distance from Rory, turning away whenever he saw him in the hallways at school, afraid he might offer him another ride in a stolen car. Not only did he regard him as dangerous, but even worse, he was afraid he might be tempted to join him on another joy ride. Despite himself, Tadd could not help but be a little sympathetic to Rory, sharing his envy of those people who always seemed to get whatever they wanted.

Later that evening, as Quine got ready to put away the Terraplane, he asked Tadd if he would like to drive it over to the trailer.

"Are you kidding?"

He smiled cagily. "I assume you have a learner's permit, don't you?"

"I sure do," he sputtered. "Do you want to see it?"

"No, I believe you, son," he said, handing him the keys. "Now let's go for a drive."

Scarcely able to contain his excitement, Tadd started the engine and slipped the car into gear, released the brake, and slowly edged ahead, gripping the steering wheel so tightly the bones in his fingers shone through his skin. The car was light and easy to handle, much easier, he believed, than the clunky Buick his father drove.

"You can take it around the fairground a few times, if you want."

"I do."

"But step on it a little, son. My grandmother drives her old Kaiser faster than this."

He pressed the accelerator lightly, and the car lurched ahead, its tires crunching across the gravel. He swung through the main gate, past the idle Ferris wheel, moving into third gear.

"I can hardly believe I'm really doing this, driving the car that Dillinger used to make getaways in from all those bank robberies."

"You haven't robbed anything, have you, son?"

Tadd was startled by the question. "Of course not. What makes you ask that?"

"Well, then, you better slow down some because you're starting to drive as fast as a bank robber."

"Whatever you say," Tadd laughed. "You're the boss."

After work tonight, Tadd had intended to tell Quine

about Rory and the possibility he might try to take the car for a joy ride. But now he was afraid that Quine, thinking he was a friend of Rory's, might no longer want him around the car, deciding he attracted a bad element from his school. He might not of course, indeed he might be very grateful for the warning, but Tadd didn't want to risk the chance of being let go because he hoped to drive the Terraplane again. There were only a couple more days left before the fair closed, and then Quine and his precious car would be gone for another year. Consequently there was no point in saying anything now, he told himself, he would just have to keep an eye out for Rory and deal with him as he saw fit.

There was no sign of Rory the next evening. Tadd was surprised, sure he would return to the fairground. Indeed, he had waited for him nearly the entire evening behind a large tool shed, out of view of the crowd around the platform, so that he could stop him if he tried to get inside the car.

He was glad he didn't say anything to Quine about Rory because later that night he again got to drive the Terraplane. Quine not only let him drive it around the fairground but even let him take it up the brown hill behind the main gate. He crept warily up the narrow, twisting road, but on the way down Quine let him pick up the pace, confident they had the road to themselves at this hour of the night. Soon they were roaring down the hillside, pretending they were being pursued by a carload of policemen, laughing until their voices were hoarse.

"God, I love this car, son. It makes me feel like—"

"Dillinger?"

"Oh, hell no," he gasped, still laughing. "It makes me feel like you . . . a kid again."

The following evening, shortly before closing, Tadd spotted Rory at the back of the crowd listening to Quine describe the time when Dillinger supposedly broke out of jail with a wooden gun. His head pulsed with fear. Quickly he stepped from behind the shed and strode toward the crowd, intending to confront Rory, but he left before Tadd could talk with him.

Tonight's the night, he thought to himself. He's coming after the car tonight.

Once again Tadd considered warning Quine but hesitated, deciding it was his responsibility to take care of the getaway car, even after the fair closed for the evening. Besides, he was still concerned that Quine would laugh at him, dismissing him as the victim of a youthful imagination. He didn't know Rory, of course, so he could not understand the sort of thing he was capable of doing. If someone dared Rory to jump off a bridge, he would ask which one, then go ahead and do it. Tadd knew that, just as he knew Rory would be coming tonight.

After locking the car in the trailer, Tadd always put the keys in the left side pocket of Quine's old red baseball jacket. Tonight, however, he kept the keys, deliberately dropping in his house keys as if he had made a mistake. He waited until Quine left for his motel room and then he sneaked back onto the fairground. He had decided to watch the car all night, making sure Rory did not take it out for a joy ride.

He curled up on the back seat, a small blanket wrapped around his shoulders. It was a warm night so he was not concerned about catching cold. And he doubted his parents would even know he was not at home, since he hadn't been coming home the past two weeks until it was quite late and, by then, they were fast asleep.

At first he was concerned he might doze off during his watch, not used to staying up all night, but he remained wide awake, jittery as a starling. He cringed at the slightest sound, the creaking of the leather upholstery, the wind in the trees, fearing it was Rory. Any moment he was afraid he would look up to see Rory at the door, trying to spring open the lock. Soon his head was throbbing, ready to burst.

Even if he caught Rory he was not sure he could prevent him from breaking into the car—he was nearly twice his size, with muscles that stretched the sleeves of his shirts. He could always hide the keys, but Rory would then hot-wire the car to get the engine started. Obviously, once he got here he was going to take the car, regardless of what measures Tadd took to stop him.

All of a sudden, before he knew what he was doing, Tadd climbed into the front seat and slid the key into the ignition. Abruptly the engine roared, seemingly loud enough to be heard by Quine in his motel room. Realizing what he was up to, he hesitated a moment, but only for a moment, then released the brake and eased the car off the trailer.

He crept past the game booths, anxiously looking all around for Rory and his friends, and as he passed through the main gate he began to accelerate. He was alone in the car and he could scarcely believe it, even glancing at himself in the mirror to make sure it was really so. Soon he was tearing across the empty road that led from the fairground, the steering wheel shaking in his hands. In moments he was climbing the hill he and Quine had driven up the past two nights. Rory would never find the car up there, he was sure, no one would tonight. And he squealed with delight, briefly sticking his head out the window.

He raced down the hillside, through the winding turns, just as he had with Quine. But now he drove much faster than he had before, pushing the antique car until its running boards rattled. His heart was in his throat he was going so fast, the tires squealing like monkeys in a cage. His face was flushed with excitement.

He started back up the hill so he could come down again even faster, wondering what Quine would think if he saw him now in his car. Possibly he would conclude he was on just the kind of joy ride that Tadd was so intent on preventing Rory from taking in the Terraplane. It was not the same thing, not at all, he tried to persuade himself, suspecting Quine would not believe him.

Abruptly he pulled over to the side of the road and turned off the engine. He continued to grip the steering wheel, staring at the silver key in the ignition, resisting the temptation to turn it and climb the hill again. Instead he decided to wait there until sunrise, when he would return the car to the trailer, figuring neither Rory or Quine would be at the fairground that early in the morning. As he sat there, trying to stay awake, he again tried to convince himself that he had only taken the car to prevent Rory from taking it. He was not making a getaway of his own as he was afraid it appeared, but even he began to have his doubts, his pulse racing with fear.

Nighttime

The door to the bedroom whispered open and suddenly the shadow of someone moved across the room, past the collage of pennants on the walls, and approached Tadd. He shuddered, imagining he was dreaming, and woke with a start, finding the figure above him, staring. Quickly he glanced to see if he had left the window open, remembering how his grandfather always believed that dreams came in through the windows at night. But it was closed.

"Wake up, Tadd." It was his mother, touching his left arm, peeling away the bedspread. "We're going next door for the night."

He groaned, then rolled over on his side and drew the blankets back up around his throat.

"Come on, dear," she whispered. "Do you hear me?"

"Uh-uh," he muttered.

"Wake up now. You've got to hurry and get dressed."

He started to ask why but already knew the answer, having heard his parents quarrelling in his sleep, so he got up and docilely pulled on a sweater and some jeans over his pajamas. The room was frigid. Then he slumped against the bookcase, still sluggish, and slowly rubbed the sleep from his eyes. Anxiously he stared at the closed bedroom door across the hallway where he could hear his parents arguing. His heart was pounding so hard, he pressed the heel of his hand against his ribs to stifle the sound. Urgently he bent over his brother and whispered, "Get up, Tobie. We're going." In a moment the door across the hallway sprang open; he could just make out the shadow of his father at the edge of the bed before his mother hurried into their room.

"Are you ready?" she asked.

"Yes."

"Now be quiet and we'll go out the back door."

They picked up their pillows and followed her out of the room, down the dark hallway, and into the kitchen. The house was quiet. A copper bowl on the counter gleamed in a shaft of light from the street. She turned around a moment, hesitating, then opened the back door and ushered them onto the porch. "I called Miss Laurel and she said she'd be happy to have us spend the night with her. You know how lonely it is for her in that big house."

"Alma! . . . Alma!" they heard their father shout from somewhere in the house. "I want to talk to you."

The boys, frightened, stood paralyzed, staring back at the hallway, until their mother coaxed them outside, saying, "Now hurry. I'll be with you in a minute."

Quickly they tore down the porch steps into the night. They streaked around the garage, across a corner of the lawn, and started down the driveway. All the houses along the street were dark, it was so late, and Tadd was glad that no one could see them running around at this time of night. For a split second, Tobie looked back and saw their father in the kitchen window, then looked away, sweating with fear. "Come on," Tadd urged him, pulling his hand as though it were the handle to a wagon. They turned at the end of the hedge that bordered their house, their footsteps whispering on the grass, and raced across Miss Laurel's parking. They ran up her bank, through the leaves, and up the porch, almost out of breath, and pressed the doorbell.

Miss Laurel, smiling tautly, pushed back the screen, saying, "Oh, come inside, children, before you turn into icicles." Her white hair, always pinned into a bun in the daytime, hung loosely across her shoulders. "It's so nice of you to come over and visit me," she told them.

They had stayed overnight before and, as in the past, she had prepared the davenport for them to sleep on, one at each end, and drawn it near the fireplace. The logs sighed and crackled. The boys quickly huddled together in front of the fire, snug in Navajo blankets, and stared at the flames. They were entranced by her fires, regarded them as magical the way the pinecones burst into green and orange and blue sparks. As they lay there, growing warm again, Miss Laurel sat between them with her photograph album as she often did when they came over and showed them pictures from her days as a young schoolteacher on an Indian reservation, reminiscing easily about those times as if they had occurred just the other week. Tadd only half believed her when she said she was the smiling young woman in the faded photographs, scarcely recognizing any resemblance to the person they knew as their next door neighbor. And once, when he expressed some doubt, she smiled the carefree smile of the woman in the photographs and admitted her appearance had changed over the years, adding, with the same smile, that she would always remain ahead of time because she had been born a year before the turn of the century. But how could anyone change so much? he wondered. How could these two people be the same person? He remained skeptical despite what she said, but still he enjoyed listening to her reminiscences about the Indians she had taught on the reservation and looking at the photographs she had taken. He wished that the night would never end, they could stay over forever in front of her fire, also ahead of time.

One summer, while still in high school, Tadd began to spend a couple of nights out of the week downtown at a small ecumenical center sponsored by the diocese and run by students from the university. It was located in a dreary corner of the city, in the cellar of a decrepit old tobacco shop along the riverfront. A slim blue cross, twisted out of tin, hung above the doorway. It was referred to invariably as the "Cellar" by almost everyone associated with it, including the chaplain. The center was something of a house church, offering services every night and providing food and counseling for the transients in the vicinity. Tadd mainly did menial work down there, scrubbing floors and washing dishes, following the example of one of his teachers at school, Mr. Nichols. Just recently having graduated from the university, where he had served as a volunteer at the center, Mr. Nichols encouraged many of the students to donate some of their spare time and help out at the center. Still single, he was there almost every night, doing everything except celebrate Mass, and Tadd often helped him prepare the musty place for the service, arranging the folding chairs around the twin cardtables that served as the altar, setting out the bread and wine, distributing the missals. He frequently cited Thoreau to Tadd during his first few weeks there, urging him to read his journals. He even had tacked a large photograph of Thoreau on the back wall, and during the service would sit beneath it on the floor and read excerpts from the journals as part of the liturgy. After a while he began to refer to Teilhard de Chardin frequently, citing him as he had Thoreau, and later Orwell and others, finding someone different every few weeks. By the end of the summer the wall was covered with photographs of his sources.

Mr. Nichols was something of an eccentric, even at school, where once he had some of his classes simulate physical injuries so that they could better understand the difficulties of the handicapped. Tadd had hobbled around on crutches for several hours while others assumed a whole range of disabilities, including Mr. Nichols, who rode around in a wheelchair all day. Tadd was not particularly surprised, then, when he appeared one night at the Cellar in torn clothes, with a trace of a beard, and explained he wanted to move around the streets as one of the transients so that he might appreciate their problems. He cited the advice of Paul: "With the Jews I live like a Jew, to win the Jews." Eventually Tadd asked him if he could accompany him on one of his walks through the district, and he agreed so long as he wore some old clothes and didn't shave for a few days.

"You can become my shadow," he said, grinning.

They set out together a week later. It was a cold, violet night. Tightly Tadd held the collar of his jacket around his throat, his head bowed, trailing half a step behind Mr.

Nichols as if he really were his shadow. He scarcely exchanged a word with Tadd at first, almost seemed to have forgotten that he was at his side as they left the Cellar. They walked cautiously down the sour streets, past taverns and missions and secondhand stores, then across the boulevard, past more squalid buildings. A few tramps milled on the sidewalks, muttering to themselves; others lingered in doorways and against the sides of buildings. Mr. Nichols, pretending he was Orwell down and out in Paris, led Tadd into every grim little corner of the district. They wandered through an arcade, visited a tattoo parlor, drank gritty cups of coffee in a Korean café, lingered with some men outside a gutted pawnshop, browsed inside the lobby of a rooming house. They stood and listened to an evangelist band playing "Amazing Grace" on a bleak streetcorner. At another corner, a whore in a light brown raincoat stepped beside them, whistling, and asked if they wanted to have a night on the town, while two figures swore at one another in front of a steambath across the street.

Tadd was puzzled at how reticent Mr. Nichols remained during the walk. He had expected him to be trying to minister to the needs of everyone they saw, inquiring about their troubles and inviting them down to the Cellar. Instead, he moved through the streets as if in a trance, seemingly oblivious to the people they passed, and Tadd began to wonder about his purpose in taking the walk. Finally, on the way back, he asked him why he had not spoken to a single person.

"Oh," he said, surprised. "I'm looking for someone."

"Down here?"

He shrugged tiredly and explained how he had come

across a young girl begging in the street a week ago and had bought her some coffee and talked with her for a while about some of her problems at home. He had agreed to meet her the following night but she never appeared. "Ever since then, I've been coming down here looking for her."

"Do you think you'll ever find her again?"

"I don't know. But I've nothing better to do than try. I'm not so different, really, than many of the people down here wandering the streets, trying to buy time for themselves. Maybe you aren't either. And I suppose there's nothing wrong with that if time is all that remains on the shelf," he said, sounding like Celine.

Tadd denied that was his motive but Mr. Nichols only smiled, and they returned in silence.

At the end of the summer the chaplain at the Cellar invited Tadd to spend a weekend at the Benedictine seminary with half a dozen other boys from the diocese. He invited him into his office one night after the service, poured him a cup of strong Turkish coffee, and extended the invitation.

"You are at the age now, Rudyard," he began gravely, touching his fingers together in a bridge underneath his sagging chin, "for a young man to start thinking seriously about his vocation. What he aspires to do with his life."

"Yes, sir."

"No doubt, like all young people, you have considered numerous avenues. Perhaps even the priesthood."

"Yes, I have, Father."

He nodded. "It has been some time since anyone from here has entered the seminary but this is not surprising. Only a few people are ever chosen for the religious life. To receive that call is, surely, the highest privilege Our

Lord Jesus Christ can grant an individual."

Tadd, listening, stood quietly before the slouched priest.

"Maybe, son, He has chosen you to serve Him. So I thought you might be interested in visiting the seminary to help you determine if that is His intention."

The seminary, composed of a cluster of modest frame buildings, was nestled in some rolling hills downstate, approximately an hour by car from the city. Tadd rose in darkness the first morning there to the sound of bells ringing in the chapel and accompanied the seminarians to the early service, then enjoyed a large breakfast in the refectory. Afterward, he was shown around the premises by one of the older seminarians who wore a black cassock, red socks, and cracked leather sandals. It was a crisp September morning. Patches of sunlight glimmered through the cobblestoned sky. They walked slowly across the immaculate grounds, past the refectory, then along a narrow gravel path, past the library and the auditorium. The sound of voices chanting in Latin floated from the windows. They continued along the path to a small grove of trees, chatting quietly together about the demands of being a seminarian, and came to the shrine to the Virgin Mother. A monk, meditating, crept through the shadows in silence. Tadd stared at him, momentarily trying to picture himself in his place. Then they climbed a grassy slope to the firehouse, where the seminarians maintained a fire engine to serve the entire community. Tadd spent the remainder of the morning there, talking with the crew, listening to them play esoteric passages of medieval religious music on a guitar they passed among one another. In the afternoon he accompanied the crew on a drive through the hills in the fire engine, observed an hour of

silence in his room, and helped some second year seminarians rake the grounds before retiring with them to the
dormitory, where he solicited their impressions of their
first year. He inquired about their daily routine, the
sacrifices they were required to make, about the difficulty
of their decision to enter the seminary. Some had known
for half their lives, others in just the last year or two, a few
continued to be in doubt. One young man, the nephew
of a Jesuit, admitted he had never been sure, even though
he and his family had always assumed he would follow the
example of his uncle, so finally one afternoon he spread a
deck of playing cards across the kitchen table and drew a
single card, deciding if he picked one of the red suit he
would enter the Army, the black suit the priesthood. He
drew a spade.

"It was sheer chance," he said. "But I guess, at times,
one has to be willing to risk even the most important
decisions on the draw of a card."

"Someone has been reading his *Pensées*," one of the
others chided. "No more blackjack with him."

He smiled coyly and removed a crumpled playing card
from his wallet. "This is the card. The three of spades."

Tadd listened carefully, sometimes probing the seminarians to help him with his own decision, right up until
it was time for dinner. After benediction, he went upstairs
to his room, intending to go to bed early because of the
small amount of sleep he had last night. But sleep eluded
him as he tossed anxiously in bed, despite how tired he
felt. He continued to be agitated by what he had observed
during the long day, desperately tried to come to a decision
about his future. His mind was a nest of nerves. At length,
he got up and went downstairs to the chapel. Only a red

sanctuary light burned in the darkness. Genuflecting, he slipped into one of the side benches, crossing himself. If he was going to brood all night about his future, he reckoned, he might as well do so in church where he could petition for some direction. At once he tried to rid every concern, every shred of thought from his mind, to make it absolutely blank, hoping to receive some guidance in his decision about entering the seminary. But after a few moments his attention wandered, and he became distracted by two monks he noticed at the communion railing, their heads in their hands, bent in supplication. Intently he watched them, once again imagining himself in their place. He could not deny the appeal of the priesthood at times. Frequently, during Mass, he pictured himself on the altar as the celebrant, lifting his hands in prayer, changing the bread and wine into the Body and Blood of Christ. And always the thought of being up there made him tremble with humility, convinced he was not worthy of being invested with such power. He marveled at how still the monks were, absorbed in adoration like the statues at the entrance to the chapel. He admired their discipline and piety yet, recalling some of the priests he had known, he suspected they must be very lonely and frightened men. Pensively he sank his face in his hands. He hated to admit it but often he felt lonely and scared, too, so he assumed he could easily adapt to the secure, disciplined life of the priesthood. Probably he would relish it, and he wondered if this was the primary appeal of the priesthood for him rather than the opportunity to serve the church—indeed, if it might not be an admission of weakness to enter the seminary, and if he had the strength to resist the temptation. He would be a fraud, his vows counterfeit, if he ever became a priest, he decided.

Silently, after another moment, he rose and left the chapel, realizing he did not belong there with the two monks.

It was close to midnight. Tadd sat on the edge of his bed, listening to his parents arguing in the kitchen, while he tried to complete a letter to Tobie who was away at school. Rain clattered on the roof. He tried hard not to listen to them but, as usual, he could hear every word, his father angrily demanding his dinner, his mother refusing. He wished it would rain harder, louder, obliterating their voices. Sweat trickled down the sides of his arms. He was seething inside and abruptly leaned back on the bed and clamped his ears with his hands. Through the oval window he could see across the street to the playground. A firelight burned by the slide. Then, turning away, he glimpsed his profile in shadow and hooked two fingers behind his head, turning himself into a gargoyle. Staring back out the window, he doubted if they would ever stop, they had been arguing with one another for as long as he could remember, their invectives echoing in every room in the house. And again he tried not to listen and resumed writing his letter.

He heard a door slam in the hallway, his father shouting, then another door. "Oh, Christ!" he railed bitterly. He sprang from the bed and tore down the stairs into the living room, where he saw his father peering into the fireplace, his face flushed. Suddenly, astonishingly, he struck his father hard across the side of the mouth. His father slammed against the wall. Terrified, Tadd thought the whole house was going to collapse, wall after wall, into clouds of dust.

Tadd leaned over the railing of the footbridge, staring at the circus caravan on the street. The murmur of the animals was exciting, fierce. Kneeling, he set his camera down on the railing and peered through the viewer, aimed, and snapped a photograph of an enormous African elephant swaying in the lamplight. Then he peered again, snapping one photograph after another as the animals were assembled along the street for the procession across the river to the Coliseum. He was strictly a novice, though he went out a couple of nights a week with his camera, snapping whatever struck his curiosity. He always wanted to be where the apples were falling, as Mr. Nichols said once, at disasters and spectacles, and over the last year he had snapped pictures of a burning warehouse, some nasty traffic accidents, a beauty pageant, numerous basketball and football games. Mostly, though, he remained in the neighborhood, snapping pictures of cars and gardens and homes. Sometimes, bored, he even took pictures of himself, making faces in a mirror, approaching a store window. He seldom expressed much satisfaction with his pictures, often neglected even to develop many of them, because more than anything the camera was simply an excuse to get away from the house for a while at night, away from all the quarrelling.

An attractive girl in a maroon dress sauntered past the lion cage, her long hair wandering down her shoulders. Tadd peered at her through his camera a moment and began to follow her, nudging through the crowd. He wanted to take her picture; often he took pictures of people he saw on the street. She was standing beside a

miniature horse, stroking its neck, when he approached
and snapped her picture. She blushed and he snapped her
again, then she insisted he let her take his picture, and he
did, smiling with surprise.

"Are you on vacation?" she asked.

"No."

"You're not Japanese, are you?"

He laughed. "My camera maybe, not me."

They introduced themselves, Tadd offered her a
cigarette, and they chatted a few moments about the
animals. Along with the rest of the crowd they followed
the procession across the bridge, continuing to become
acquainted. Lisa lived downtown in an apartment with
her spinster aunt, was already out of high school, and in
another year intended to enter nursing school. Later, over
coffee, Tadd told her about going out at night with his
camera and described some of the pictures he had taken,
especially the fires. She admitted she was also something
of a night owl and recalled the belief of her aunt that
everybody had a particular time of the day that suited
them as surely as a shade or color or a band of automobile.
On the bus she sometimes tried to identify the character-
istic hours of other passengers, associating, for instance,
the early hours of morning with brooding people—
sleepwalkers, she explained; sunrise with the vigorous and
athletic; midnight with the violent; the late afternoon with
idle people with little ambition. As she gazed around the
blue café, she began to ascribe certain times to different
customers, saying, "She's a noontime person... she's one
in the morning . . . he's three in the afternoon." Then,
regarding Tadd, she agreed that he belonged somewhere
in the evening, the time for wanderers, she suggested,

including herself. He smiled in amusement and invited her to accompany him some night, and she accepted tentatively.

A few nights later Tadd met her downtown and they walked together along the riverfront, smoking cigarettes and snapping pictures of the large Asian freighters. At the end of the seawall, his heart shivering, he kissed her, touching her tongue. They met again the following week, strolled through Chinatown, took each other's pictures beside a storefront dragon, sipped crème de menthe in a musty coffee house. Soon they were meeting two and three nights a week, usually at the library, and would wander through some corner of the city together, holding hands. He continued to bring his camera with him but took very few pictures other than those of her, at the different places they visited. She had become his excuse for leaving the house now, not the camera.

One night, walking through the university, they heard a sudden burst of applause from behind the fieldhouse and instinctively headed in that direction. They walked around the fieldhouse, where they found a cluster of students gathered around a lopsided tower of old boxes and crates and furniture fragments, laughing and swilling beer. In a moment, several torches were tossed at the tower, igniting it into a fierce red cone. The students erupted in more applause. Tadd led Lisa through the crowd, past the bonfire, to a small slope on the other side of the field. They sat down on the grass by themselves and watched the tower burn. Lisa speculated she might enjoy going to college rather than nursing school, while Tadd dreaded the idea, detesting everything about school. She leaned back on her elbows, her lavish hair hanging loosely behind her shoulders, and predicted he would go to college. He protested, "What's really important can't be taught. It has to be learned." She smiled, leaning back farther, revealing the shape of her small breasts. The crackle of the fire whispered through the trees. She lay there absolutely still as if asleep, her eyes closed, breathing slowly. He stared at her breasts, the tiny star in her left ear, the rings on her fingers, the soft down on the back of her neck. He wanted to touch her breasts, her mouth, to bury his head in her hair. He could smell the faint scent of her perfume and delicately traced a finger along her arm. She opened her eyes, saw him staring, and leaned over and touched his cheek. He stared into her eyes, into her dreams, saw them still together, walking through strange, dark streets of other places, in other worlds, holding hands.

"This fire was only a block from the Capitol building. You can see the dome in the distance."

Tadd sat next to Lisa on a striped cushion on the floor, showing her the photographs he had taken after the riot in Washington that spring. They were at her apartment high above the street. It was Saturday afternoon, he had only been home from college a few hours, and he was still tired from the long flight he had taken last night across the country. She made him some peppermint tea and he sipped it gratefully as he described the different photographs.

"It's awful," she said, looking at a picture of smoke pouring out of a doorway.

"It used to be a hardware store."

She sighed. "It's hard to believe this is America."

Quickly he rifled through the remaining pictures and handed her one of a short, bald-headed man descending some stairs. On the phonograph dropped an album of the Doors.

"Who is he?"

"Dos Passos."

"You mean the writer?"

He smiled. "The ambulance corps . . . Paris . . . the lost generation. I found him." He snapped his picture, he explained, coming out of the university library one afternoon where he sometimes came to do research.

"He looks like a librarian."

"Everyone does, I suppose, if they live long enough."

Then he put away the snapshots, saying he was tired of looking at the past, and suddenly pulled a small camera out of his pocket and snapped her picture. She laughed and posed a moment, pushing back her hair. He snapped her profile, her back, her legs, her long hair. She undid her blouse and lifted out her left breast toward the camera, and he snapped it, and then her other breast as she let her blouse slide off her shoulders. He slid beside her on the floor, they kissed one another, and he held her in his arms. He could feel her breasts swell beneath him as she breathed. Briefly, as they embraced, he caught himself in her eyes. His face appeared strained, fierce, and he looked away in fear. They loved one another abruptly, awkwardly, searching for a rhythm, then lay together in silence, listening to the Doors.

That evening they wandered around town for a while, staring at the city lights, then walked to the courthouse. A demonstration against the war was to begin from there later, and Lisa intended to participate in the march through town. Tadd was surprised, not that she wanted to march, everybody was marching these days, but at the intensity of her anger. Just a short time ago, before he went away to school, she had seldom expressed the least interest in politics, but as they approached the courthouse she now told him about numerous other protests she had engaged in over the last six months, including her arrest for kneeling in prayer inside of the induction center. She had become obsessed with the war, like so many others their age, and he could hardly listen to her, having heard the arguments so many times already. He supposed he had grown cynical and distrustful of everyone's views—even irresponsible, according to some people who resented his detachment.

A few hundred people milled in front of the courthouse. Behind them, at the top of the steps, a few others stood over a plain black coffin, holding candles in their hands to mourn the dead in Vietnam. A squad of policemen stood with nightsticks across the street, staring at the protesters.

"Hurry," she said. "It's going to start." She pushed through the crowd, urging Tadd to follow, but he declined, considering it a waste of time.

"You go ahead. I'll watch."

She glared at him a moment, her face reddening, then turned and quickly disappeared among all the protesters. Tadd remained on the corner, peering through his camera as the march proceeded behind the truck carrying the coffin. He recognized several people he had not seen since high school, including Mr. Nichols, who resembled Che Guevara more than Orwell now with his long, scraggly hair, and snapped some of their pictures as they wound down the street into the night, chanting, "Hell, no, we won't go . . . Hell, no, we won't go . . . "

They were alone together in the house, Tadd sitting at the bedside of his father. The room was filled with the sound of his breathing. Tadd bent over him, dampening his forehead with a moist cloth, still astonished at how terrible he appeared since coming home from the hospital, his eyes bulging, his complexion dry and sallow, his cheeks sunken. Sadly he gazed out the window at the moon. His father was dying, he knew; it was only a matter of time, according to the doctors, a week, a month, only a little while longer before it happened. And since they could not provide any more treatment, they had discharged him a week ago to spend his remaining days with his family. He rolled up his father's pajama sleeve, patted his arm with cotton, and administered the injection, slowly introducing the medicine into his muscle. Then, setting the syringe on the nightstand, he rolled down his sleeve, propped up the pillows. Outside, a train rumbled through the night, its whistle blaring. His father scarcely noticed it, almost seemed asleep, although his eyes were open, staring across the dark room into the hallway. Solicitously Tadd brushed some lint from his collar, adjusted the blankets around his throat.

"Do you want anything, Dad?" he whispered, after a moment.

His father remained silent, staring into the hallway, and he doubted if he even understood him; half the time now he seemed in a daze from all the medicine he was taking. Absently he grazed his father's long, smooth fingers. They felt like porcelain, he thought as he watched him close his eyes and fall asleep. Gently Tadd held his hand, caressing his knuckles. His own hand, to his surprise, was smaller, slighter, not nearly as firm as his father's hand, which was as blunt as a baseball glove, and yet he cringed because it was this hand that he had raised against his father one dark night. The memory sickened him, and anxiously he dismissed it from his mind. Instead he recalled the long weekends he used to spend at the seaside when he was small and how his father would take him down to the beach early every morning. Gripping hands as tightly as they could, they would slowly wade into the water and jump the waves breaking across the beach, stepping farther and farther out but holding onto one another, the waves crashing against their legs. He had depended on the strength of his father's hand then, and now, pressing it against his cheek, he gripped it as though he were never going to let go, just as he had as a boy.

Airtime

"Fasten your seat belts," Trummy broke in on his theme music—"Come Fly with Me," played tonight by Count Basie and his band. "The magic carpet is set to take off."

Tadd slid back from the microphone and loosened his shoelaces, settling in for another Saturday night and Sunday morning as Trummy. This was the identity he had assumed ever since he began his stint at the listener-sponsored radio station KUKU. It was in memory of a "boneman" in the Ellington band he had always enjoyed. A couple other disk jockeys at the station worked under aliases and Tadd decided to do likewise, figuring that as someone else he'd have a lot more interesting things to impart to his audience. As Trummy, he was someone special, a trombone player who had been around the world more than once and played with nearly every important name in the field.

"As the jazzman says, 'Those who know don't say, and those who say don't know.'"

The telephone blinked as he queued up "You Go to My Head" by Louis Armstrong on the other turntable.

"KUKU, may I help you?" he answered.

"Trummy?"

"Yes, speaking."

"This is Doris," the soft voice whispered shyly. "I don't know if you remember me but I called the other week to ask to hear something by Chet Baker."

"Sure, I remember," he lied, unable to remember her request out of all the ones he had received over the past few weeks.

"Do you recall what you played?"

He hesitated. "I'm afraid you'll have to give me a hint."

"'My Funny Valentine.'"

"Do you want to hear it again?"

"Actually, I'd like to hear something where Baker sings, if that's possible?"

"I'll see what I can do."

"That was Sadao Watanabe and his quartet playing 'Star Eyes,' and before that, Bill Evans with his composition 'Waltz for Debby.' And we started off the set with 'Lady Be Good.' The long violin lines you heard there belonged to Joe Venuti, perhaps the finest jazz violinist who ever drew a bow, Stéphane Grappelli notwithstanding. I never had the pleasure to play with him but I understand he was quite a prankster. The story is probably apocryphal but it is said that out of boredom one day Venuti called up different union halls and booking agents and arranged for several dozen bass players to meet that night in front of the hotel where he was staying. And he roared with laughter as he looked down at all those musicians lugging their basses up and down the sidewalk, bumping into one another, wondering what in the world they were doing there."

Sipping coffee, he slid back from the microphone, his ankles crossed on the desk, and looked over the album notes from the Blossom Dearie record he was then playing. He not only did this to pass the time and satisfy his curiosity, but it also gave him something to tell his audience between sets. He could only read so many public service announcements, and he hated to resort to the jibes and glib remarks favored by so many of his colleagues at the station.

He envied performers like Blossom Dearie, who were blessed with the kind of talent that enabled them to visit so many different places in the world while earning their living. He'd have given anything for her talent, but his voice was scratchy as an old Vaughn Monroe 78 and all he could peck out on the piano was "As Time Goes By." Perhaps this is why he introduced himself into the careers of some of the artists he featured, pretending, as Trummy, to have played as a sideman at various recording sessions and concerts and night clubs to compensate for his own lack of talent. All he had to do was say he was somewhere and, as if by magic, he was, sliding his trombone behind some of the finest jazz musicians in the world. He slipped into the false identity he had created for his broadcasts as if it were his own, finding it fit him much more comfortably than the one that brought him to the station.

"One flew east, one flew west," Trummy intoned, "one flew over the KUKU's nest. You're listening to listener-sponsored radio—all jazz, all the time."

"Thank you for playing 'Blame It on My Youth' the other night. I really enjoyed it."

It was Doris. Tadd was not surprised he recognized her voice, which was soft and delicate as a moth, almost whispery, the kind he liked to receive when he answered the request line.

"I'm glad you liked it."

"I'm curious, you've played with so many people, did you ever play with Chet Baker?"

"Sorry, can't say that I ever did."

"That's too bad, especially since he's gone now."

"I know," he said, fidgeting with some albums scattered across the desk. "I understand he fell out of a window in some hotel in Amsterdam."

"There's talk he may have been pushed out by someone he crossed in a drug deal."

"Really?"

"That's just something I heard. I don't know anything for sure."

"I wonder if I should say anything about it on the air?"

"I wouldn't, if I were you, because it may be just loose talk. Better to play his music and let him rest in the peace he never found in his life."

"Yeah, you're probably right," he sighed. "Anything you want to hear in particular?"

"How about 'My Funny Valentine' again?"

"You got it."

"If you tell the truth," Tadd remembered his father telling him, "you only have to tell one story." But who wants to hear only one story? Not his audience, certainly.

It was miserable outside, stormy and bone-snapping cold. The wind was blowing so hard his battered old Volkswagen swayed as he drove across the bridge to the station, the rain pelting the cracked windshield. Nights like these made him wish he lived in the desert where it seldom rained a drop.

In the studio, however, it was much different, mild and carefree as a late April afternoon, as he spent nearly the entire first hour playing gentle, pastoral selections. Despite the terrible weather, he was confident he could make his audience believe it was really a lovely spring day, just like his uncle, he believed. Uncle Hays was a trial lawyer, and Tadd remembered catching him once with a cigarette after he promised to quit smoking and asking him why he broke his promise and he denied that he had, even though the cigarette was clenched between his fingers. That was his uncle all right, convinced he could persuade anyone of anything.

Toward the end of the set he played three different versions of "Spring Can Really Hang You Up the Most," hoping this would lock his audience into his make-believe spring afternoon.

Following her rendition of "God Bless the Child," Trummy said of Billie Holiday, "Once, as a child, she fell asleep in her grandmother's arms, and when she awoke her grandmother had died, and the old woman's arms were locked around her."

One of his favorite tunes was Billy Strayhorn's "Lush Life," which he played a couple of times a month, sometimes oftener, depending on his mood. Occasionally, after he played it, he recalled for his audience the story of the trumpet player who, after playing the tune the first time, went out and bought a very expensive wedding ring because, as Dexter Gordon told him once, he was tired of "playing in dives and breathing in what other people breathe out." He wished to settle down, become a teacher maybe, so whenever he saw someone he found attractive he offered her the ring, hoping she would accept it, but always it was declined. Eventually he quit making his offer and kept the ring for himself, wearing it on his pinkie like a thousand talent agents he had met over the years, resigned to continue living the lush life of a horn player.

"The moral of this story," Trummy told his audience time and again, "is that mousetraps don't chase mice."

"I might've given it serious consideration if I'd been offered that ring," Doris admitted after she heard the story.

"You would, would you?"

"Especially if it were offered by someone whose music I really liked."

"Like our friend Mr. Baker?"

"You better believe it," she answered. "And what about you, Trummy? Would you accept such a proposal if it were made to you?"

He snickered. "In the words of Buddy Holly, 'That'll Be the Day.'"

"You never know."

"Why, do you have something in mind?"

She was silent for a moment. "Play me something by Baker, please," she asked, then hung up.

"One of the shrewdest observations I ever heard was made by this Hungarian guy I was blowing with in some joint in Chicago. We had finished our last set and were packing up our horns to leave when all of a sudden he looked out at the smoky little room and said, 'I have seen the future and it is much like the present, only longer.' Sounds like something Dizzy might've said, doesn't it?"

"I don't have a ring but I might have something else you'd be interested in."

"What'd that be, Doris?"

"You'll have to come and see for yourself."

"I just went on the air. I can't go anywhere now."

"But I'm right outside, in the parking lot."

"All right," he said excitedly. "Give me a couple minutes to queue up some music."

Hurriedly he gathered together a hefty stack of records that would last a good hour of playing time, all the while thinking about another disk jockey who, last summer, reportedly accepted an invitation from a listener to come over to her apartment right during his show, which he was able to do by playing several Prestige double albums.

There was only one other car in the lot besides his and he walked over to it, his heart pounding so fiercely he was afraid it was going to burst through his chest. "Doris, is that you?" he asked as he approached the driver.

"Trummy?" she said quizzically.

He chuckled to himself. "Yes, don't you recognize my voice?"

She regarded him carefully. "You aren't anything like I'd pictured you'd be. You're so young."

"I'm not that young."

"But from all the things you've said, all the people you've played with, I figured you were at least my age, if not a little older."

"Well, I'm sorry to disappoint you."

Stiffly she swept a hand through her tangled red hair, her eyes crinkling in agitation. "You didn't play with any of those people, did you?"

"No, I didn't."

"Then why in God's name did you say you did?"

"Because I thought I'd be more interesting to my audience, I guess."

On the car radio Chet Baker began to sing "Almost Blue," but she turned it off abruptly. "You're a damn liar. That's all you are."

Anxiously he crossed his arms over his chest, hoping to keep his heart intact. "What is it you wanted to show me, Doris?"

"I thought I'd share some memories with you from the night I met Chet Baker but you probably weren't even born then."

"I'd like to hear them."

"Forget it," she snapped, cranking up the window. Quickly she started the engine and pulled past him, slowly gathering speed until all he could make out were her taillights moving down the narrow road.

"The magic carpet continues to soar," Trummy assured his audience when he returned to the studio, "but my heart is on the ground tonight. I disappointed someone this evening, getting myself 'marooned in a blizzard of lies,' as the song says. But I suppose we are the stories we tell, even the made-up ones, aren't we?"

Table Time

Whistling softly, Tadd found the spare key under the mat, slipped it into the door, and entered the dark apartment with the bouquet of violets tucked behind his back. "Hello," he called, switching on the hall light. "Anyone here?"

The refrigerator clicked in the silence.

He knew Eryn was not here, she was still at work, which was why he came at this time of the afternoon. He wanted to leave the flowers as a surprise, as something of an anniversary present, because of the marriage ceremony they had pretended to go through six months ago tonight at the Casablanca party given by her sister. He knew she would not forget despite their recent differences. With a smile he recalled himself in the borrowed white dinner jacket and Eryn in a long beaded gown and beaded cap, Eryn humming "As Time Goes By" in his ear as they danced on the terrace. Toward the end of that evening someone, insisting their night in Casablanca should have a happier ending than the film, proposed that everyone dressed as Rick and Ilsa get married, so they and several other couples exchanged vows on the lawn before smashing their champagne glasses against the garden wall and shuffling through the broken glass as if it were coarse desert sand.

He was certain that night that he and Eryn would become man and wife someday. They had been together for almost a year until a week ago, when she shocked him by suggesting they should meet some other people for a while. He could not understand how she could make such a ridiculous suggestion. He wanted her to become his wife, he didn't want to meet any other people. Incensed, he stayed away from her all last week, brooding in a different tavern every night, trying to determine what had happened between them.

He set the flowers on the walnut end table, which was cluttered with mail, and instinctively began to sort the letters into two neat stacks. He came across a large Valentine card, which seemed odd since it was October, opened it, and began to read the small slanted writing on the inside of the card. After just a few words he dropped the card on the table and suddenly sank against the wall as though he had lost his breath. The card was from a lover. Devastated, he could feel the blood draining from his face. He and Eryn had only been separated for a week, less than a week actually, he calculated to himself. How could she have found someone else already? He realized of course there must have been someone else for quite a while, someone she was seeing at the same time that she was seeing him. He was so furious he wanted to smash everything he could see in the apartment, but he could not move away from the wall. He felt pinned there, like a leaf against a fence. Idly he stared around the room, acknowledging he did not even have the strength to break the violets he brought for her.

The telephone rang repeatedly that evening. Tadd was sure it was Eryn calling to thank him for the flowers so he refused to answer it, determined to put her out of his thoughts once and for all. The telephone rang several more times the next evening while he sat next to it, sipping green Chinese tea, trying to convince himself that he never wanted to hear her voice again. But after the telephone stopped ringing late at night, he began to drive over to her apartment house, sometimes just circling the block once or twice before leaving, sometimes parking at the corner where he could observe her apartment through the elm trees.

One evening, approaching the apartment house, he spotted her stepping out of an old blue Falcon and hurriedly parked behind a panel truck as the driver helped her out of the car. At once he suspected this man was her lover, for he did not recognize the car as belonging to any of her friends. She clung to him as he walked her to the door, her arm wrapped around his waist, her head touching his shoulder, just as she used to cling to him sometimes after he brought her home. They disappeared through the doorway, and in a moment her apartment glowed with light. Tadd stared at the living room window, watching their shadows slide across the drawn curtains. Anger slowly gripped his heart. He recognized how ridiculous it was to put himself through the pain of watching Eryn with someone else, but he could not take his eyes off the window.

The telephone began to ring as Tadd opened the beer he always had as soon as he got home from the office. "Hello," he answered.

"Hello, Tadd."

It was Eryn. The sound of her voice bit through the receiver sharply, making his skin prickle with goosebumps. He started to hang up on her but instead hung on nervously, saying nothing.

"Hello? Are you still there?"

"I'm here."

"I saw you last night. I know what you're doing."

He kept silent.

"I saw you parked in front of my apartment house."

"Don't flatter yourself, Eryn," he said, trying to sound convincing.

"I know you're hurt. I can't blame you for being angry. I know I should have told you about Keith. I tried to several times, honestly, but I couldn't."

"I don't want to hear about him."

There was a short pause. "Anyway, I understand how you feel but still that doesn't mean you can spy on me at night. I'd thought you'd be more mature about what's happened between us, frankly."

"I don't know what you're talking about."

"I think you do, Tadd. And I want you to stop it. I'd hoped we could remain friends."

"Friends?" he snarled. "I didn't want to be your friend. I wanted to marry you."

"I'm sorry, Tadd. Really, I am," she said quietly and hung up.

The silence buzzed in his head.

Despite himself, he was unable to keep away and returned the next night, wanting to see her again even if it was only a glimpse of her shadow against the curtain. Not surprisingly, the blue Falcon was parked in front of her apartment house. He waited for almost an hour and a half, staring up at her window, half listening to the radio, before Keith came out and got into his car. Then, out of curiosity, he followed him, wondering where he lived, but instead of going home Keith drove to a dreary redbrick tavern near the train depot.

A middle-aged couple sat at the bar rolling dice while three other people, a man and two women, danced together to the music of Waylon Jennings that blared from the jukebox. Keith was nowhere in sight. Tadd ordered a beer and asked the bartender if he saw where he went.

"If he's not down here having the time of his life," the bartender cracked, "he's probably upstairs, shooting."

"Excuse me?"

"Pool, friend, shooting pool."

Tadd swallowed his beer and climbed the sour stairwell to what the bartender had referred to as "the shooting gallery." It was twice the size of the room downstairs with a dozen tables scattered across the dusty checkered floor. It smelled of chalk and cigar smoke and disinfectant. A remnant of a bar stretched along one wall, against which some men leaned, their cue sticks braced against their sides, watching others play at the tables. They seemed as intent as Tadd reckoned he must have appeared a little earlier tonight staring up at Eryn's apartment, seemed as lonely too, he thought, as he made his way toward them.

"You lookin' for a game?" a portly man with a smudge of blue chalk on the tip of his chin asked disinterestedly, as though it were his turn to ask.

"No. Just looking tonight."

He saw Keith crouched over the corner table with a

bridge, carefully lining up a shot. His suit jacket was folded over the back of a chair, his shirtsleeves rolled to his elbows, his tie tucked inside the front of his shirt. A cigarette burned on the corner of the table. Practicing, he slid the cue back and forth a moment, then smoothly banked the shot in and proceeded to sink every ball on the table. His opponent stuffed some dollar bills into a corner pocket and walked away as Keith racked the balls.

"He's a shooter," the man beside Tadd remarked, tapping his stick.

"He ain't bad," the portly man said, grudgingly.

"He's as good as this place deserves on a Tuesday night."

"I can't argue with you there."

Along with the two old hands, Tadd watched Keith practice some two-rail bank shots, sinking one after another with a crisp, firm stroke, although he was less interested in watching his performance at the table than he was in watching him. Inevitably he compared himself with Keith, trying to determine precisely what it was about him that Eryn found so attractive. Not a particularly handsome man, he had pale, thinning hair and a prominent nose. His brown eyes, large as walnuts, shone through his steel-rimmed glasses. Probably it was his confidence that attracted Eryn, Tadd thought, the belief that he could accomplish almost anything if he set his mind to it. Plainly, in a roomful of people Keith would consider himself at least the equal of anyone there, while Tadd seldom would, even when only one other person remained in the room. He supposed the only thing he had ever really learned from his father was fear, which gripped him like the claws of some ponderous bird, so that all his life he had been shy and diffident. This fear was what he despised the most about himself. Absurdly, he hoped to conceal it from Eryn, acting as if his shyness were really indifference or arrogance, but he knew it was only a matter of time before she saw through his disguise.

Intently he watched Keith lean across the table, aim, and sink another ball, envying his confidence, wishing he could be like him, just once.

On an impulse, driving to Eryn's the next evening, Tadd headed instead to the tavern where he had followed Keith. He did not see the blue Falcon out front but decided to go in anyway, ordered a beer, and went upstairs to the shooting gallery, which was still as cold and musty as the other night. Two of the men he had noticed leaning against the bar then were still there, watching the tables, their expressions unchanged. He stood beside them for a moment, wondering if Keith would appear, then he decided to shoot some balls. He picked out a stick and walked over to one of the tables in the back. Idly he grazed the palm of his right hand over the smooth baize surface, remembering the many Saturday nights he and his friends from high school used to spend at the bowling alley, drinking green rivers and shooting pool on a lopsided old table by the equipment counter.

He racked the balls into a tight triangle, carefully took aim, sliding the stick back and forth across his thumb, and fired, barely breaking the balls with his soft, awkward stroke. His game needed some work, he thought to himself, smiling. Methodically, then, he played against himself, solids against stripes, slowly clearing the table until only the eight ball remained. Neither side won, really, one just lost sooner than the other. He racked the balls again and played a second game, which took him nearly as long to finish as the first one, and then he called it a night. On the way home he drove past the apartment house, where he saw the Falcon parked at the corner. The two long games he played had left him too depleted to stake out Eryn tonight so he continued on home.

A couple of evenings later, after he watched Eryn leave with Keith, he returned to the gallery and played at a table until midnight. He came back the next night, played until closing, then the next night and the night after that, continuing into the following week. He was becoming as much of a regular as the old hands who leaned against the bar every night. Though he was reluctant to admit it, he hoped to become proficient enough so that one night he could challenge Keith to a match and beat him, thinking that might provide him some solace.

Tadd's improvement was slow but steady, so that at the end of most nights he felt as if he had gained something, unlike at the office where it seemed as if he were on a treadmill going nowhere. For a while he was content simply to play against himself, practicing the shots that had proven the most troublesome to him, declining the occasional offers for a game, but after a few weeks, after he began to gain some confidence in himself, he agreed to play some of the old hands for table time. The games were surprisingly competitive, with him coming out on top nearly half the time.

"You're getting touch to handle," Scoey, one of the better players among the regulars, told him after Tadd nearly beat him late one night.

"Luck," he said modestly.

"Luck nothing. I've watched you coming in here at

night, putting in your time at the tables. You've earned what you've done."

"Maybe."

"You have, believe me. So many wrong numbers drift in here night after night, lose all they've got in their pockets, and you never see 'em again. But you've had the orneriness not to be shaken off the tree. And as long as a person has patience he can always improve. Believe me, I know."

Tadd believed him all right, he knew his game had improved significantly since he started going to the gallery, but he knew he had to improve even further before he could square off against Keith. Quite a few times Keith had asked him if he wanted a game, as he asked everyone when he sauntered into the room, but Tadd invariably declined, knowing he offered no serious competition for him yet and not wanting to lose to him a second time. If he played him he wanted to beat him, to crush him as if he were an insect beneath his thumb.

Whenever Keith was at the gallery Tadd watched him closely, trying to emulate his smooth stroke. Often after he left Tadd would replay some of the more difficult shots he made. But he hated it when Keith deliberately showed up someone as he liked to do sometimes, no doubt because he saw himself as that person, and could not comprehend how Eryn could care for someone that cruel. But maybe she had seen only the admirable qualities Keith had demonstrated at the table, the acuteness of his concentration, the confidence he exuded as he played, the excitement he engendered. Maybe she had yet to see what he could be like at other times at the table. One day she would, though, Tadd was sure. One day she would confront a stranger.

"You want to shoot some nine-ball?"

Tadd looked up at the tall, straggly man standing at the other end of the table, fingering the stubble on his chin. "Sure, I'm game."

The man gathered the balls into the triangle. "Shoot for ten dollars?"

"Let's just play for table time."

"Jesus, man, I need some incentive when I play. I'm sure you've got ten dollars in your wallet."

Tadd chalked his cue. "All right, forget it then."

The straggly man glared at him a moment, anxiously fingering his chin, then turned and smiled at his girlfriend who was sitting along the wall sipping a drink. "Then table time it is, man."

A quarter was tossed to see who would break, and the man won and broke the balls furiously, sinking the five ball but leaving most of the others bunched against the cushion. His first shot, a short bank shot, he sank into a side pocket and leaned back confidently, chalking his cue. Tadd was not concerned, though; he knew he was the better player after the first shot because the man had neglected to set up his next shot. Instead, he left the cue ball buried in a corner. After he missed, as Tadd knew he would, he stared at his girlfriend in disbelief, groaning something about the surface of the table.

Tadd expected such lame excuses from him so he was not surprised. Almost as soon as the straggly man stepped through the doorway, Tadd felt an intense dislike toward him because of the way he swaggered around the room, running his hands over the different tables as if they were not good enough for someone of his caliber. Seething, he watched the man's posturing in front of his girlfriend as he made some simple trick shots that appeared difficult, noticed how her eyes were riveted on him, shining each time he sank a shot. And the thought suddenly entered his mind that Keith would behave in much the same way if he ever brought Eryn along with him some evening, carrying on as if he were better than anyone else, although in his case he would probably be right.

Now he decided to make him realize he was not as good as he or his girlfriend believed. Lining up his shot, he reckoned he could probably clear the table right away and be finished with this game, but instead he missed the shot, deliberately burying the cue ball against the cushion. Scowling, the man missed again, and so did Tadd, after taking a long time to shoot. He had decided to play very slowly, suspecting this would irritate the man, and took his time on every shot, concentrating not on making any of them but on leaving the cue ball in as poor a lie as he could. A few old hands gathered around the table, amused at the apparent inability of either of them to sink a shot. Soon the man began to seethe, complaining angrily to his girlfriend about the slowness of the game. And as if to rebuke Tadd for his deliberateness he rushed his own shots, scarcely even lining them up before shooting. The tactic worked just as Tadd hoped it would; after several minutes the table remained covered with balls and the man was rattled, his patience spent. He began to complain more loudly, grimaced at the derisive looks he received from the old hands around the table.

"Jesus Christ," he snarled at one point after Tadd missed an easy tap-in, "I don't have all night to waste on this game."

"Do you want to concede?" Tadd asked calmly.

"Hell, no, I intend to win, man."

Someone snickered.

Tadd continued to miss for a few more minutes until the man seemed thoroughly frustrated. Then he drilled in a short bank shot, then another, sinking all his balls in a matter of moments. Fuming, the other man had blood in his eye.

"You think you're pretty clever, don't you, mister?"

"Do I?"

He stared coldly at Tadd, saying not a word, staring so coldly Tadd had to turn away. Then he strode past the grinning crowd, muttering under his breath, with his girlfriend trailing after him, listening.

A few of the old hands congratulated Tadd on his performance.

"You took him apart," Scoey told Tadd, "piece by pathetic piece."

"Like clockwork."

"I guess you've learned something up here, after all."

"I guess so," Tadd said lamely, his eyes still averted.

"Here, let me buy you a beer," Scoey said. "You deserve one, my boy."

"No, another time. I've got to be going."

"Gracious, it's early, sport. It hasn't been dark an hour yet."

Tadd turned and walked away slowly, silently, leaving his cue stick on the table, and went outside to his car. It was a cold, clear night. He started to open the door, then paused and braced himself against the hood as if his knees were going to buckle. He was breathing heavily. Sickened, he felt as if he had been turned inside out, exposed, wished he could disappear somewhere. He was appalled at what he had done tonight, swore to himself he would never return to the gallery again. He played tonight just as Keith had all those times when he toyed with his opponents, he humiliated the straggly man, and he disliked himself for it just as he did Keith; more so even, he supposed, since he realized what he was doing almost from the moment he began the game. He knew in his heart he could never become skilled enough to defeat Keith, so when the man asked him to play he pretended this perfect stranger was Keith, thinking that by humiliating him he could gain some satisfaction for what Keith had done to him, restore some of the confidence he had lost after losing Eryn. Instead, though, he felt disgusted and ashamed, knowing he had embarrassed himself as much as he had his opponent, knowing he had become someone he disdained.

Later, driving home, he swung past Eryn's apartment house, although he did not stop or even glance up at her window. Still, he came back, and he knew it would take a long time to forget her, just as it would take a long time to forget tonight.

Another Time

The streets were filling with cars when Frances picked up Tobie at the office. On Wednesdays she kept the car to go to her macramé class at the church. Tired, Tobie was happy to let his wife drive him home tonight and slumped back in the seat, staring idly out the window at the fuming traffic. It had been a long day. Shortly the light mist that had fallen all afternoon turned into a heavy downpour. He wished, as he gazed out the window, that the rainy streets were swimming pools and that he and Frances could go swimming together as they had last summer when they visited some friends in Nevada. He was so tired of the rain, he swore sometimes he was going to move to the desert to live one of these days. He clasped his hands behind his head, inhaling the light scent of Frances' perfume, remembering the night they swam without any clothes on in their friends' pool and made love on the lawn.

Up ahead, in the middle of a long, cluttered block, a string quartet played Mozart in front of a partially restored old firehouse, and as they drove past them Tobie suddenly thought he saw Elaine among the throng of people walking along the sidewalk. "Get into the inside lane," he snapped at his wife.

"What for?"

"I thought I saw someone I knew."

He watched her move through the crush of people, trying to catch another glimpse of her face, to be sure she really was Elaine. At the corner she turned down the block beside an obese man carrying a lemon-striped umbrella.

"Turn right," he said.

"But that's not the way home."

"Hurry, please."

She swerved down the side street, bristling. "Who is it you think you saw?"

He searched both sides of the street but he could not see her anywhere. "Goddamn it," he railed. "She's vanished."

"Who, Tobie?"

"Someone I used to know. You don't know her." He brooded a moment, surveying the people. "Let's circle the block."

"But look at the time," she protested. "Pretty soon we won't be able to budge, the streets will be so crowded. Can't you call the person on the telephone later?"

"All right, don't then. I'll walk."

"Oh, don't be ridiculous, Tobie."

Abruptly he opened the door, stepped out of the car, and splashed across the street, dodging traffic. Then he ambled slowly behind a smiling girl selling chrysanthemums, carefully looking all around for Elaine, touching himself to make sure he was not dreaming that he was searching for her again. Quickly his clothes were drenched in the soaking rain. He peered through storefront windows, stepped into an antique shop thinking she might be in there, described her to a doorman outside a hotel and asked if he had seen her. At length, returning to the corner where he had seen her last, he stood beneath the awning of a jewelry store and scrutinized everyone who walked around the corner. But she never appeared and he began to wonder if he had only seen her in his mind, as he had so many times before over the past few years. When it grew dark he took a taxi home, feeling just as Frances said he would, ridiculous.

He resumed the search for Elaine the next day during his lunch hour, walking around the same reeking block until his shoes felt as heavy as shovels. Diligently, the rest of the week, he searched for her during lunch and after work, knowing how ridiculous he must have appeared going down there all the time, wandering the street like some vagrant. He suspected he might not have even seen her, or if he had he would not see her again, but still he went down there on the slender hope that he might see her one afternoon. Despite his marriage, he was still infatuated with Elaine.

Nearly five years ago, Tobie had worked one summer with Elaine in a dilapidated little neighborhood theater that revived old American films. She worked behind the refreshment counter, pouring chilled cider and bitter Turkish coffee, while he sold tickets and handed out solemn little introductions he had culled from James Agee's criticism on the films that were shown. They both were in their last year of college, looking forward to graduation, and often during the screenings would sit at the chessboard in the lobby and confide their aspirations to one another. Soon he thought about little else when he was away from the theater than returning and spending the evening alone with her in the lobby, listening to her talk. He had other girlfriends, even one he had thought about marrying, but none of them affected him like Elaine. She made him feel agitated when he was away from her during the day, made him dread the weekends when they were not working, so that frequently he would ask her to go out with him on Saturday night. She seldom accepted, but when she did he would always take her downtown for a drive so that some of his friends could see her sitting beside him in the car. He wanted to show her off because he knew they would not believe someone as attractive as her would go out with him. Even he found it hard to believe sometimes, because she was as lovely as any of the women in the films screened at the theater.

Some nights when they went out together they would make believe they were various performers they saw on the screen. Elaine, he remembered, especially liked to be Veronica Lake, often she swept her flashing blond hair across the side of her face, spoke in a soft, lazy drawl, and smoked cigarettes through a tortoiseshell holder. One evening, driving downtown together, they pretended they were Alan Ladd and Veronica Lake, exchanging fragments of dialogue they remembered from recent screenings of *The Blue Dahlia* and *This Gun for Hire*, nervously looking behind them for dangerous men lurking in the shadows.

As much as she wanted to be Veronica Lake, Elaine also wanted to be an elder cousin she corresponded with who worked as a secretary at the American embassy in Paris. After graduation, she was determined to visit Paris, maybe even attend the Sorbonne for a semester, and travel through Europe, visiting museums and drinking wine.

Politely Tobie listened to her describe the itinerary she had made out for her trip, even though he was not particularly interested in Paris or the Sorbonne or travelling around Europe. He tried to seem interested because she was so interested but he could not conceal his indifference. She knew him too well, much better than he knew her, he suspected.

"You're not very ambitious, are you?" she said to him one evening while she was discussing her itinerary.

"Of course I am," he said, surprised.

"I mean, you're not interested ever in going anywhere … in leaving here. You're content to stay here for the rest of your life."

He shrugged. "It's my home, isn't it?"

Gradually she seemed to grow distant toward him, scarcely speaking to him sometimes, always having an excuse why she could not see him on the weekend. He became distraught, afraid that he was losing her. He worried that he was not ambitious enough for her because he did not want to travel overseas. Desperately, then, he became someone other than himself at night at the theater, just as he had when he became Alan Ladd, pretending now that he was interested in travelling to all corners of the globe, trying to impress upon her his ambitiousness.

Finally, gathering his nerve, he confronted her one evening to find out why she was ignoring him. She acted as if nothing was wrong at first, but as he persisted in demanding an explanation, she admitted she was in love with someone else, a Paraguayan in his third year of medical school. Even though he suspected there was another person in her life, he was still stunned by her admission. Anxiously he tried to tell her how much he loved her, how he had intended to ask her to marry him after he graduated, but she refused to listen and clamped her hands over her ears. Ashamed, angry, he slumped over the chessboard, paralyzed with rejection. He sat there the rest of the evening, brooding to himself, not going home until early in the morning. Outside, on the corner, he saw an empty wine bottle, picked it up, and smashed it against the side of the theater, convinced his life was as shattered now as the broken glass at his feet.

Elaine was startled at how badly he reacted to the knowledge that she loved someone else. He seldom exchanged a word with her anymore, always appeared haggard and gaunt, moved around the theater as if half asleep. She became alarmed at his behavior, and during her last week at the theater she told him if he still wished to see her he could drive her home from school a couple of times a week. He accepted her offer and for three months picked her up and drove her home. Sometimes, after dropping her off on Friday nights, he would park his car around the corner and watch the medical student come by an hour later to take her out for the evening. Once he even followed them around for a while, becoming the mysterious stranger he and Elaine often fantasized was shadowing them when they pretended they were Alan Ladd and Veronica Lake. It was humiliating. After he met Frances, he continued to drive Elaine home for a few more weeks then stopped, realizing how pathetic he must have appeared to Frances. He resolved to forget Elaine then, imagined she had perished in a terrible fire he had seen blazing downtown one afternoon, but this was impossible because he loved her more than anyone he had ever known, including Frances. And despite the pain her memory evoked, he knew he could never forget her, however many fires he imagined burning inside his head.

Driving home, Tobie as usual circled the reeking block before crossing the river, still searching for Elaine. For the past six days he had been coming down here, and he wondered how much longer to continue the search. Another day? Another week? It seemed hopeless, like searching for a coin at the bottom of the sea, he thought, as he stared at all the people walking along the street. He was tired and bored, ready for a drink. Frances had started to ask him why he was coming home late every night, suspicious that he was playing cards again he supposed. He did not dare tell her he was still looking for Elaine because he was afraid she might become jealous or, more likely, think he was being foolish, so he let her think he was gambling with some fellows from the office.

Around the corner, leaning against the smeared window of a pawnshop, an old woman stared at him, her long, seamed face smiling in recognition. She was always standing there and he looked away in apprehension, feeling as if he were becoming as much of a vagrant as she was by coming down here so often.

Suddenly there Elaine was, stepping out of a tanning salon, her blond hair shining in the long afternoon light. His heart turned over excitedly. He closed his eyes for a moment, half expecting her to be gone when he opened them, but she was still there. Amazed, he signaled and turned the car into the inside lane, following her as she strode through the crowd. As he approached her, he rolled down his window to offer her a ride home as he used to do at school, but instead he stared at her without uttering a word. He began to perspire under his arms. Then, abruptly, he accelerated and raced past her and headed toward the bridge. He told himself he did not say anything to her because he thought she might be someone else, but in his heart he knew she was Elaine. Just as he knew he had kept silent because he was afraid she would reject him again.

He smiled as he drove across the bridge, thinking how it was just like Elaine to go to a tanning salon in the dead of winter. She was always so concerned about her appearance.

The next day he called and made an appointment at the salon, hoping he might run into Elaine there. Thinking about her all night, he decided it would be best to confront her face to face to see if she would acknowledge him, otherwise she could always pretend she did not notice him if he just called her name while circling the block in his car. He had never dreamed of going to a tanning salon before, regarding such establishments as frivolous and the people who frequented them as shallow and vain, so he was a little jittery when he entered the place. Tahitian music floated softly from a speaker on the floor. The receptionist who took his credit card, a nutbrown woman with a flowered lei around her neck, handed him a bottle of sunscreen and directed him through a beaded curtain to the sixth sun room. He anticipated running into Elaine at any moment as he followed the woman, but no one else appeared in the corridor. Maybe later, he thought, as he stepped out of his clothes in the anteroom and folded them into a wire basket.

The sun room was sweltering, the lemon walls and ceiling radiant with long vertical lights. He daubed himself with sunscreen and stretched out on the cool ice blue bed in the middle of the room. Casually he looked at himself, at his pale stomach, his even paler legs, trying to picture himself becoming as brown as the receptionist. He grinned: he was as pale as a ghost. Quickly he began to melt in the appalling heat, felt as if his bones were turning to butter, but after a minute he relaxed on the bed and closed his eyes, imagining he was lying on the beach of some tropical island a thousand miles away. For a moment he imagined Elaine lying beside him on the beach, her hand in his, her head nestled against his shoulder. He grimaced a little, thinking of all the exotic places he had seen them at together in his mind. He was astonished he saw her the other week, astonished too that he saw her again yesterday, because he had understood she had married a lawyer and moved to Los Angeles a few years ago. But he was not surprised he recognized her after all this time. He knew he could never forget her—not in thirty years. At night he would often think about her before falling asleep, hoping that he would dream about her.

Maybe beauty is the beast, he thought to himself as he watched his skin redden under the glaring lights.

He left the salon without seeing Elaine, so he returned the following afternoon, but still he did not see her even though he waited quite a while in the lobby before leaving. He considered forgetting the whole idea, but instead he came every afternoon that week to the salon. Slowly he adjusted to the intense heat of the room, and even more slowly he began to brown, turning the shade of caramel by the end of the week. Increasingly, before going to bed at night, he closed the bathroom door and admired his darkening complexion in the mirror. He hated to admit it, but he was glad he had not run into Elaine yet because he did not want her to see him until he was brown as a walnut.

"You're getting so dark," Frances marveled one evening as he undressed for bed. "Are you coming down with a rash?"

"I've been going to a tanning salon."

"You're kidding."

"No, I'm serious."

"Whatever for?" she asked, surprised. "Why do you want a tan?"

He folded his trousers, set his shoes in the closet, thinking of an explanation. "Someone at the office asked me to go along with him so I did," he lied. "He's leaving for the islands in a couple of weeks and he wanted a tan so he didn't look like a snowman on the beach."

She regarded him a moment as he did his knee-bends at the foot of the bed. "You look a little Japanese, Tobie, if you want my opinion."

Around the middle of next week, as he was leaving the salon, Tobie saw Elaine leaning over the reception desk with her back to him, talking on the telephone. He hesitated a moment. As she hung up the receiver he approached the desk, wondering if she would recognize him after all these years. She seemed to be looking straight through him, through the oval window by the door, and as he stood next to her she said nothing. His heart throbbed heavily and noisily, sounding as loud as the rain rattling against the awning. Impulsively he turned toward her and said, "Excuse me?"

"Yes?"

"I believe we know one another. My name is Tobie Rudyard."

Her china-blue eyes shone coldly as she looked at him. "Sorry," she said. "I don't remember."

Tobie was indignant, convinced she was only pretending not to recognize him, but he controlled his temper. "We worked together one summer at the old Orpheum theater."

"Oh, of course," she said, after a moment. "Forgive me. But it's been a while."

"Five years."

She nodded, staring again out the streaming window.

"How have you been?" he asked hurriedly, trying not to let the conversation lapse. "The last I heard, you were living in California, in Los Angeles as I remember."

"I was. Then my husband and I separated, and I moved back up here about three months ago." She snickered, fingering an earring. "But I didn't want to lose my California tan so I've been coming here a couple of times a week since it started raining."

"And here we are, together again . . . after five years."

"Small world."

"An attic."

She touched his wrist. "Or an old movie theater."

Smiling, he asked her to have a drink with him but she declined, saying that she was waiting for a taxi. He persisted, however, offering to drive her home later, and she accompanied him around the corner to a crowded little lounge simmering with the taped music of the Modern Jazz Quartet. They sat at a table in a corner, their faces quivering in the candlelight. An artificial fan turned slowly overhead. They tried to compare their tans but it was too dark inside the lounge. Tobie, noticing all the rings on her fingers, asked if they were just worn for decoration or if they each held a special meaning.

Elaine leaned forward and raised her left hand against the candlelight. The rings gleamed. She touched the turquoise stone on her index finger, explaining that a friend had won this for her at a shooting gallery in Long Beach one night. She passed over her wedding band to the emerald on her middle finger, which she said had belonged to her grandmother who brought it with her when she came to America from Budapest. On her small finger was a speck of a diamond she had been given by an architect she had lived with for a year after her first marriage dissolved. Tobie was surprised to learn that she had been married more than once, and even more surprised that she had taken a lover, considering her religious background. The rings on her right hand also were from other men she had met in California, and he grew jealous as she described some of her affairs. Then, as she spoke about the person who gave her the jade ring on her middle finger, her eyes suddenly began to tear. She had become pregnant by him and had had an abortion because she thought she would lose him if she had the child.

"Then he left anyway. The bastard."

Startled, Tobie placed his finger against her lips, not wanting to hear any more about what had happened to her in California, to have the impression he had carried of her in his mind all these years spoiled any further. Gently he scraped a cloud of hair across the side of her face and whispered, "Veronica Lake."

"Who?"

"The actress. Don't you remember? You used to comb your hair like hers at the theater some nights."

She dried her eyes, smiling faintly. "Oh, I'd forgotten."

"I didn't," he said shyly. "You could have been her sister. You looked just like her then. You still do."

Driving her home, he started to tell her about his infatuation, describing how he still dreamed of her at night, how he looked for her in every girl he had gone out with since he met her. She seemed not in the least surprised about his revelation, as though she had heard others reveal similar feelings about her, and after a minute he stopped because he was afraid she might regard him as not any different from the men she had known in California. And he was certain he was not like any of them, he cared for her too much, he could never leave her as they had, so he kept quiet and let her talk about her plans to return to California in the summer.

In front of her apartment house, sitting a moment in the car, she leaned across the seat and kissed him on the cheek. Then she invited him up to her apartment, offering him some sherry. He knew he could have her now, but then he would be like all the others who had had her, he realized, so he declined the invitation. He wanted to preserve her in his mind as a dream, someone absolutely perfect, rather than as this woman sitting beside him in the car who was asking him up to her apartment.

"Another time, maybe," he said.

"Promise?"

"I promise."

She unlocked the car door. "I'm sorry but I've forgotten your last name. I have such a pitiful memory, I am afraid."

"Ladd," he said, turning on the motor. "Like the actor."

Swingtime

Always, as soon as Tobie set foot inside the cramped little shack known as the "Dugout," he felt as if he had slipped back into a place that he thought was only preserved in a corner of his imagination. Glancing around the shack, he felt half his age, a boy again whose single interest in life was baseball.

The walls were plastered with pennants from all the current franchises in the Major Leagues as well as some obsolete ones, with yellowed photographs of legends like Honus Wagner and Tris Speaker and Rogers Hornsby. The air smelled of rosin because of the clump of bags on sale at the end of the counter. And mingled with the smell of rosin was the cherry-scented pipe tobacco blend smoked by Alec, the proprietor of the Dugout, who sat near the middle of the counter, talking with a customer.

Alec was in his late fifties, with a corona of coarse white hair that seeped out from under the old St. Louis Browns cap he was wearing. He wore a different cap nearly every day, advertising his merchandise. Casually he nodded as Tobie walked over to the bat rack along the far wall. "Here to take some swings?" he asked.

Tobie grinned faintly. "Still want to see if I have my

eye, I guess."

"That's something easy to lose all right, even for the best of hitters."

He noticed, as Alec was speaking, that his right wrist was wrapped in an elastic bandage. "What happened to your hand? You get in the way of a knuckleball or something?"

He grimaced. "Hell, at my age, as Stan Musial said once, a person can get hurt just standing around."

Tobie laughed and picked from the rack the 32-ounce black Louisville Slugger he had used the last couple of times he was here to take batting practice. Most of the bats in the rack were aluminum, and those felt alien in his hands as cricket bats, because when he grew up playing baseball all bats were made of wood. Once he took a few cuts with one of the aluminum bats, but the sound it made as it struck a ball was a dull plink that he associated less with the game of baseball than with leaded bottles falling off a shelf onto the floor. It was a strange, flat, curious sound that was absolutely foreign to the diamonds he had played on as a youngster.

After paying Alec, he shouldered the black bat and went outside to the batting cages. There were half a dozen of them, stretched in a ragged row to the right of the shack. The first two cages were occupied by a couple of American Legion players with strong shoulders and even stronger wrists who were ripping line drives to all fields. Shyly he stepped past them, wondering if they were wondering what someone his age was doing out there, and headed to the last cage. He was old enough to be their father, he thought to himself, almost in disbelief.

Before stepping into the cage, he removed his suit

jacket and folded it on the bench, tucked his necktie inside his shirt and rolled up his sleeves. Briefly he leaned against the bench, stretching his legs. Then, balancing the bat across his shoulders, he twisted slowly from side to side, trying to get limber.

"You hit that one right at the shortstop," one of the boys hollered to the other, laughing.

"Not a chance."

"You did too."

"I hit 'em where they ain't," the other boy insisted, recalling the famous maxim of Wee Willie Keeler.

Trying to ignore their chatter, Tobie assumed his stance and began to swing the bat, slowly and methodically, at imaginary fastballs crossing the middle of the plate. He felt relaxed, strong, sure of himself. Once he got in the cage, he was confident he'd pound one line drive after another out of the infield. "Streaks of lightning," as an old coach of his used to call them.

When he was the age of the boys in the first two cages, there was scarcely anything he liked to do more than hit, especially when he was in one of those grooves when the ball seemed as large as a grapefruit as it came across the plate. He was a pretty good contact hitter in his day, if he did say so himself, but now his day was gone of course. He was not a kid anymore, able to play baseball all summer long. He had a wife and daughter to look after and support, with responsibilities those two boys hadn't even thought about yet in their young lives. Still, he enjoyed taking batting practice almost as much as he did when he was their age, perhaps because he could pretend things were again as carefree as they had seemed when he was a boy.

His arms limber, he entered the cage and took a deep breath, trying to silence the bees swarming inside his stomach. Carefully he planted his feet in the batter's box, the left one first, digging his right toe into the dirt. Then he started to touch the tip of his bat on the edge of home plate but quickly drew it back, remembering the concern of Ted Williams that the bat might collect some dirt and then become heavier. Cocking his wrists, he settled into his stance, ready to swing.

The first pitch thrown by the machine was a fastball over the plate and he pulled it down the third base line. The next pitch was letter high and he snapped his wrists and fouled it off the screen. He nailed the next three pitches, however, surely pounding one for extra bases. He smiled with satisfaction, hitting the ball where it was pitched, just as he had tried to do when he played American Legion ball.

He was introduced to the Dugout nearly seven months ago by Ralph, who played second base for his old Legion team. The place had only been open a few weeks then and one Saturday afternoon, as a lark, Ralph suggested they go over and take some cuts. Somewhat reluctantly he agreed, despite not having swung a bat in years. And to his surprise his eye remained sharp, and quickly he began making solid contact with the ball, hitting it hard and deep. Before long, both of them seemed as sure of their skills as ever and even did some situation hitting, taking turns at trying to hit the ball where the other one said it should be hit. To his delight, Tobie won a pitcher of beer afterward because his hitting was a little more accurate than Ralph's.

"Back back back back back back," one of the boys

stammered as the ball arced across the pale blue sky and headed over the left field wall. "Gone!" At once the two boys erupted into cheers, making it sound as if their entire team were huddled around their cages.

Home run hitters are tyrants, Tobie believed, defining everything in terms of sheer power. Not like him and Ralph, who were content to hit the ball where the situation demanded it be hit.

Grimacing, he lowered his right shoulder and lined the ball into what would have been the hole between first and second. He smiled, recalling another coach of his who used to say, time and again, "God gets you to the plate but once you're there you're on your own."

Although he had been to the cages numerous times, he had never returned with Ralph but always came alone—usually when he was in a bleak mood, worrying about something or other. Certainly it was preferable to sitting in some bar and drinking himself into oblivion. In the cages he became so absorbed with hitting that he didn't have time to brood on whatever was bothering him. He had to stay alert or else he might swing at a ball and miss.

"Damn," he swore as he chopped a little bleeder along the foul line.

He was out here just last Thursday and hit for an hour, trying to forget an angry exchange he had at work with his supervisor. And over the past few weeks he found himself in the cages after quarreling with his wife, after receiving another speeding ticket, and after losing quite a bit of money at the racetrack. This was where he often came when he sought refuge from his tribulations, a place of concealment and rest where he could forget what was gnawing at him.

Any moment now, Tobie figured, slicing a foul ball, the service at the church would be over. Then everyone there would be on their way to the cemetery, their clothes reeking of incense and smoke, the smell of the church probably remaining with them for at least a couple of days.

He was also supposed to be at the funeral of Matty Sisler, an old friend from high school, had even received permission from his supervisor to take the afternoon off in order to be there. He wore his dark blue linen suit today, along with a sedate burgundy tie. His shoes were gleaming. And he was on his way to the service when all of a sudden he decided not to cross over the bridge to town and instead swung around and drove to the batting cages.

Matty took his own life, dying in his car from carbon monoxide poisoning. Tobie was shocked when he learned of his death. It had been nearly a year since he last saw him, but it was hard to believe he could have grown so despondent in that time as to do what he did. He had always seemed so vibrant and full of promise, never one to take less than the most from what was offered to him. He even whispered at the top of his voice.

Tobie came to the cages because he didn't want to think about what had happened to his old friend. There, he hoped he would become so engrossed in hitting baseballs that he would not be able to dwell on the sad and despairing thoughts that he was sure would torment him at the service. Besides, the person who did what Matty did wasn't anyone he knew in high school, he rationalized, so there was no point in thinking about someone who had become a stranger. And for a while he managed to keep Matty out of his thoughts as he concentrated on getting good wood on the baseballs sizzling across the corners of the plate. His eyes became dark smudges. Soon his shirt became dark with sweat, clinging to his back and shoulders. An airplane grumbled overhead, but he scarcely noticed it.

He was pleased with his efforts today in the cage, thought he was stroking the bat as well as he had in a long time. His swing was fluid and compact, with some sting behind it for a change. He hit a few short, lazy balls in the air but mostly he was cracking line drives into the outfield.

After a while, despite his resistance, Matty began to intrude on his thoughts, particularly when he nailed a ball deep into center field. Then he imagined his old friend chasing it down and snaring it in the web of his cracked yellow glove, just as he had done so many times when he played center field on the same Legion team as Tobie and Ralph. Curiously, Tobie didn't mind the intrusions and after a while even began to encourage them, picturing his friend running after more and more of the balls he hit into the outfield. He figured it was more appropriate to pay his final respects to Matty inside the cage than at the church or cemetery, because here he was able to remember him when he was young and strong and seldom made any mistakes.

And so, by the end of the afternoon, nearly every time he got good wood on the ball, he saw Matty again, roaming across center field with the sun in his eyes.

Pastime

Tadd stands in the middle of the driveway with one leg crossed in front of the other, slowly bending toward the ground until he touches his toes, pauses for a moment, then just as slowly unbends himself, only to bend again through several repetitions. His breath floats in front of him, dense as smoke. Idly he watches the Fletcher family across the street climb into their station wagon to go to church and waves at them as they drive past, still stretching. The cathedral bell rings faintly in the distance. Repeatedly he twists into a knot, stretching his hamstrings until they are loose. Then, sighing, he shakes out his arms, staring up at the softly falling rain.

"You running again, Mr. Rudyard?"

He looks around and sees the Moffet boy slowing down on his bicycle, also on his way to church, apparently, from the tie and jacket he is wearing. "Hello, Timmy."

"Where are you running today? Around the lake again?"

He smiles, rotating his shoulders. "Home."

The boy frowns, puzzled. "You're already there."

"My old home. Where I lived when I was your age."

"Is that very far away?"

He broods, not exactly sure. "Across the river and then

another mile or so."

"Almost a marathon."

"Almost," he replies, stepping across the leaves on his lawn to the sidewalk and casually beginning to run down the street, prickling with sweat, at a slow, even pace.

He used to run distance in school but had not run a step since then until a few months ago, when some fellows at the office coaxed him into running with them at noon. The first time, he dropped out after the third block, his lungs searing, and swore he would never run another step again. But he was back running in a couple days, trailing far behind, and continued to go out with them every other afternoon as they crisscrossed the city. In time he developed his endurance enough to stay with them, stride for stride, and before long he began to overtake them, leaving them behind eventually. It was a challenge, he supposed. He was tired of standing still, never really accomplishing anything, and he began to run every day, even entered some road races, finishing deep in the pack. Now he is preparing to run in a marathon at the end of the month. For the past four weeks, he has been logging more and more mileage, almost fifty miles the last week. On Sunday he always goes on an extended run, to adjust himself to running a long distance over a considerable length of time, and during the week the notion came to him that running back to his old neighborhood would be a good training run. It promises to be farther than any of his previous distances. Otherwise he has no reason for going back there, after all these years; it is just a distance whose direction he knows.

As he runs he calculates that he has not been back to his old neighborhood in seven years, since the funeral of his next door neighbor, Miss Laurel. He is surprised. It seems twice as long, somehow. And until then, he had not returned since he moved away with his mother and brother after his father died, nearly four years earlier. There was no point to going back, really, as so many of their friends had also left by then, except for Miss Laurel. A descendant of trail walkers, she would never leave, as she often told people. This is where her family crossed the country to live, often she had shown him photographs of those young men and women who had walked the Oregon Trail, she could never move. This was their home.

He runs a mile to the water tower, climbs a small slope, scattering some crows, and runs along a grassy boulevard that winds down the middle of the street. It is so early in the morning he is practically alone as he runs past the old frame houses, like a ghost, the sound of his steps silently absorbed by the fallen leaves. He is hardly breathing. Approaching a row of cars parked along the curb, he catches a glimpse of himself striding by in one of the windows, a pale thin shadow. A shock of hair rises chaotically from the back of his scalp. His shoulders are bent, his head also, his bare legs are as thin and ashen as sticks of chalk. He almost buckles with laughter, he appears so ridiculous, someone his age running through the street torturing himself, and is relieved it is so early out that no one else can see what he sees in the car windows. During the week, running with people from work, he seldom felt self-conscious, but now he realizes how foolish he appears, a fraud, seemingly trying to be a child again. And, accelerating, he streaks past the rest of the cars, refusing to look at himself anymore, and surges across the street through a vault of larch trees. Then, silently, he cautions himself to slow down so he will not be too tired to finish. There's no fire, there's plenty of time.

A block ahead of him, a woman on a bicycle wavers into view, pedaling an infant, and he wonders if he can keep up with her, lengthening his stride, but gradually she disappears through the trees. Then he is by himself again and eases into a more natural pace. Often, running alone, he picks out people along the way to race against, to distract himself from the pain the pounding creates along his shins. Generally they have no inkling they are involved in a contest as he tries to catch them from behind or at least stay even with them. It is a race with only one competitor; only he knows if he loses or succeeds. Although, smiling, he recalls an incident a few Sundays ago while running the loop around the lake when he passed another runner, an older man in a yellow windbreaker, only to be passed by him a few moments later. Tacitly they raced down the hill, the shadow of one another, until Tadd reached his car and stopped, his chest swelling. The older man continued on in silence, with a slight turn of his head to acknowledge the competition. He was old enough to be his father, Tadd remembers, even though his father never lived long enough to be that old. At the time he was embarrassed that the older man had stayed with him through the entire descent; then he came to see him as someone to admire, at his age running so well and hard, an incentive perhaps as he prepares for the marathon. Maybe he is not so ridiculous after all, he thinks.

Crossing a rickety footbridge, he trudges up a trail of black mud to the crest of a hill, then begins the long descent toward the river. The sun rises through a frayed cloud, leaving the hillside in shadows. Winding along the side of the road, he approaches a stretch of clearing and slows to look down at the roiling river and the tall city buildings in the distance. Somewhere along here his grandfather used to bring him and his brother on Saturday afternoons to watch the ships slide up the river to the seawall. And he remembers once his grandfather telling them of the time, when he was their age, he had learned there was a black man aboard one of the ships, and every morning for a week he sat at the end of the seawall waiting for him to appear because he had never seen a black person before. He enjoyed coming up there more than either of the boys did, recalling memories and ambitions of his childhood. Often he predicted that both of them someday would sail somewhere far away, unlike him, but like him both of them remained behind, watching others come and go as he had once watched the black man.

As he descends, the buildings downtown seem to rise toward him, becoming larger, more detailed, almost as though he could reach out and touch them with his hands. Randomly he notices the Congregational Tower, the library, the Hilton, a revolving milk sign, the Pioneer Courthouse. He knows every street, every building, having lived here most of his life, and can spot places without even looking at them. He marvels at how little the city has changed over the years, too little perhaps, revealing the conviction among many of the citizens that people are welcome to visit but not to stay. Sometimes he wonders why he remains, thinking of himself as stranded in this remote corner, a castaway abandoned to his imagination. "Don't think you have to be like everyone else, with nowhere to go," his grandfather declared once as they stood along the hillside. "See a part of the globe." And consequently he has been around the world, twice—seeing the ruins in Yucatan, swimming in the Aegean, wandering through Westminster Abbey, visiting the shrine at Lourdes.

Strange, he thinks, how easy it is to remember things that never happened.

He runs along the riverfront for half a mile, surging up a spiral ramp onto the old trestle bridge. Cars swish by ominously within inches of him. A passenger in a yellow convertible heckles him, hollering, "Faster... faster." He ignores her, accustomed to being heckled when he runs. He has heard everything seemingly, had things tossed at him—apple cores, stones, cartons of milk. Once, running in the park, a truck swerved at him, its driver convulsing with laughter as he sprinted for safety.

The smell of tar hangs heavily in the chill air, mingling with the rank brackish smell of the river. At the end of the bridge, to his surprise, a road crew is patching some holes on one of the approaches. The smell is part of his past, invariably evoking in his mind the playground in his old neighborhood. When he was very small, he remembers, it was just a dusty, sloped stretch of weeds adjacent to the schoolhouse, where he fought dragons and knights with a wooden sword and a paper shield. Then, early one morning in the summer, a crew of workers suddenly appeared and stayed for the rest of the week blacktopping the playground, obliterating all his secret hiding places, making the slope smooth as slate. The smell of the blacktop seemed to pervade the neighborhood for weeks, possibly years, and he can still see himself standing across the street, watching them spread the steaming dark liquid into an immense square that later was enclosed in a link fence and divided into a baseball diamond and a football field with white and yellow lines. He was very upset at first, though quickly he came to adjust and play organized games with the other children of the neighborhood. Even now he associates the scent of tar with the erasure of a particular world that he inhabited alone, a wilderness of imaginary adventures.

Someone briefly counts cadence, "Hut, two, three, four," from a passing van.

He has gone almost five miles so far and he feels surprisingly strong still, relaxes and takes a deep breath, shaking his arms along his sides. Confidently he watches himself as he approaches a tavern window, becoming larger and larger, convinced he can run the marathon tomorrow. Passing the tavern, he abruptly makes a sharp turn and circles back toward the river to look for the Groggery, a place he occasionally frequented in college, and finds it has been turned into a real estate office with color photographs of white homes for sale in the windows. A Closed sign hangs on the door and, curiously, he jogs up to the office, peering up at the blank ceiling. Every year after graduation, there was a signing day there when the graduates came in and, stretching from table tops and chairs, signed their names across the ceiling. By the time he graduated it was black with signatures and predictions. He smiles, recalling all his ambitions then, the ambitions of some of his friends; school is invariably the time you think you are better than you are, he supposes. He scrawled his name in the lower right corner somewhere, and years later he brought his wife there and she stood on his shoulders and signed her name next to his, in violet ink. He wonders if she even remembers this place; probably not, he suspects. It was so long ago, fourteen years in June. The past to her is something you leave, like a foreign country. She grew up in a small resort community in the mountains but whenever they are in the vicinity she declines any suggestion of returning there. "Why go back to a ghost town when there is everything ahead to see?" she snapped at him once. Something of a fatalist, he does not share her anticipation of what lies in store for them, becoming increasingly suspicious that a person is only going to have one direction unfold before him. The future to him, at times, seems as inviolable as the past.

He is beginning to feel the distance, a slight stitch is developing on his right side, and he reduces his stride a little, approaching the stone gates that mark the entrance to the neighborhood. "Not much farther," he consoles himself, aloud. His arms are sleeved with sweat, and he lets them hang a moment by his sides, dripping.

Across the street, a small black girl races ahead of him to the end of the block, pulling a clattering string toy along the pavement. He smiles at her but she stares at him impassively as he turns the corner and runs across the intersection, scattering more birds. Away from the noise and congestion along the riverfront, he can begin to hear himself as he runs, his breathing, the slap of his shoes, a bone clicking in his left knee, sounding like the circus coming to town, he thinks, half expecting to look up and discover someone in every house pressed to a window to see who is making all the commotion. He passes the Riordan place and recalls the pile of stones they kept in their milk box to throw at any dogs that wandered into their yard. He winds through an alley between an apartment building, passes the home of an old girlfriend, where a cluster of young faces appear in the front window staring at him, laughing. Surprisingly, the houses appear much as he remembers them appearing, except for some different shades of color. He expected them to have diminished somehow, but they have remained remarkably the same, so that he almost feels as if he could step inside any one of them and find—still there—the people he remembers living there. Coming to the old Sheed place, he glances at the small oval window in the kitchen, the apparition of Mrs. Sheed waving at him as he crosses her driveway. It is as if he never left, seemingly; the run back here is more than just a distance, another part of his preparation for the marathon, he realizes. He has returned in time as well.

Instinctively he follows part of his old newspaper route, which takes him down a narrow side street into the park, where he startles a derelict asleep on a bench, past a nursery school with paper pumpkins in the windows, and up to the church. Strains of an organ carry through the parted windows. The parking lot is full of cars, and he slows, listening to the congregation sing, remembering, as a youngster, singing the same hymn, although in Latin. The last time he was here, at Miss Laurel's funeral, the church was practically empty as she had outlived most of her close friends. The only person he recognized was Father Strand, whom he used to serve Mass for as an altar boy.

"I understand you've moved out of the parish," he said to him after the service.

"Yes, Father."

"Across the river?"

"Yes," he said, almost apologetically.

The old priest nodded. "It is only natural that one moves away. Home is the cradle and people can't remain in the cradle forever. Don't become a stranger, though. One shouldn't forget where they came from. There is nothing wrong with paying a visit, now and again. And you don't have to wait for another funeral to return."

"I won't," he assured him, touching the priest on the arm.

He trudges across the playground, aching, a little startled to see that a corner of the baseball diamond has become a deep hole, surrounded by shards of blacktop. As it used to be, he thinks, peering down at the red mud. At the end of the next block will be his old house, framed by two immense oak trees. He slows down almost to a walk, holds his breath, silencing himself for a moment, as he approaches the green house on the corner. Gradually it emerges through the mist, the squat chimney, the winding steps, the long white porch, the details coming together piece by piece to confirm his memory. But for a moment, so far away, it is difficult to determine if there is a house there anymore, as he can make out only a dim brown shadow ahead of him, which is reminiscent of the old photograph Miss Laurel had of the yard before his parents built a house there. Then it was a large vegetable garden, with rows of potatoes and squash and beans and peas and lettuce, which the few people who lived in the neighborhood then had planted because of the Second World War. Miss Laurel described it as a victory garden. He remembers, sometimes, finding a potato sprouting from the flowerbeds and taking it in to his mother to prepare for dinner, just for him. It was as though he had found gold, he was so excited.

He stands in front of the house, slumped in exhaustion. He grips his sides, breathing heavily, furious because he thought he was in better condition. His calves are tight as coils, his heart pounds, his arms and legs ache. He is shocked he is so tired. Astonishingly, it takes a slight effort for him just to raise his head, but when he does he is just as amazed at how little the house has changed; a deeper shade of green, a clutter of cardboard boxes on the porch, otherwise it is much as it was when he moved away. Curiously he wanders around the corner of the house and pauses in the breezeway, gazing over the fence at the cookstove he helped his father build one summer in the backyard. Some bricks at the base of the stove are loose, in need of repair, he notices with concern, as if he still lives there. A shovel and a rake lean against the stove in the rain, turning to rust. Thirsty, he crosses the lawn to the faucet by the back door, turns it on, and scoops handfuls of the metallic water into his mouth, swallowing noisily.

"Is there something I can do for you, mister?"

Tadd looks up and sees a swollen man in an undershirt and gray slacks standing in the doorway. His chin is covered with shaving lather, flecks appear on his cheeks and ears. "I was thirsty," he tells him.

The man glowers behind the screen. "You're trespassing, you know."

Tadd starts to tell him he used to live here but decides not to and says, "I've been running."

"Where are you running to?"

"Home."

"Is it far?"

"Far enough."

"Well, then, I guess you better be on your way."

He nods, turns off the faucet, and leaves the resident standing in the doorway.

He intended to visit Miss Laurel's house next door, but instead he jogs back down the street toward the playground. The new resident is right, in a sense, he is trespassing by returning here. It is another world. Though there is but one world, most people live in worlds of their own, and once this was his world but not any longer. Now it belongs to others.

Crossing the playground in pain, he suddenly feels ridiculous again, almost wishes he could hide somewhere, and does, by imagining the time when this too will be a memory as his old neighborhood was once a memory.

Acknowledgments

Excerpts from this work have been previously published in *The Acorn, Aethlon, Arete, Beloit Fiction Journal, The Burnside Reader, Cynic Magazine, The Fiction Primer, Freight Train, Lake Street Review, Liturgical Credo, The Monocacy Valley Review, Red Cedar Review, Ripples, The Square Table, TQR, The Ultimate Writer, Unirod, Unknowns,* and *Words of Wisdom.*

About the Author

T. R. HEALY was born and raised in the Pacific Northwest. He is the author of three novels, *Ancient Shadows, Caught in the Cold Snows,* and *Red Weather,* and a collection of stories, *Partial Survivors.*